100

YOUNG
VISITOR
TO MARS

OTHER BOOKS IN THE

YOUNG
HEROES
LIBRARY

YOUNG SIOUX WARRIOR

YOUNG SAND HILLS COWBOY

YOUNG PONY EXPRESS RIDER

YOUNG VISITOR TO MARS

YOUNG BUCKSKIN SPY

YOUNG INFIELD ROOKIE

YOUNG HERO OF THE RANGE

A Young Heroes Library Volume

YOUNG VISITOR TO MARS

By

RICHARD M. ELAM, Jr.

ILLUSTRATED BY CHARLES H. GEER

GROSSET & DUNLAP

NEW YORK

Library of Congress Catalog Card Number: 53-10375

Contents

Contents

List of Illustrations

CHAPTER ONE

Beyond the Earth

THE ROCKET SHIP *Shooting Star* powered through the black deeps of space like a silver bullet. Inside a room of their parents' suite aboard the vessel, Ted Kenton and his sister Jill sat before a large window looking out at the wonders of space in the year A.D. 2003.

"It doesn't seem as if we're moving at all, does it, Sis?" Ted asked.

Jill shook her auburn head. "No, but it scares me to know how fast we're going!" she replied.

Ted straightened his sturdy young shoulders and shook strands of brown hair out of his eyes. It was natural that girls should be scared of things

9

connected with space travel, he thought. "Thousands of miles an hour isn't much," he said lightly.

"But what if we should hit something!" Jill complained. "It would be an awful crash!"

"The only things we have to worry about hitting are meteors," Ted told her. "The *Shooting Star* has radar instruments that tell us when they're headed straight at us."

"Father says that sometimes meteors come so fast that space ships can't get out of the way of them," Jill returned, with solemn eyes.

In brotherly fashion Ted pressed the shoulder of his eleven-and-a-half-year-old sister, younger than he by a year. "Don't start worrying about everything that can happen to us, Jill. We've got a lot ahead of us on Mars," he advised.

"I—I'm not so sure I want to go to Mars," Jill blurted. "It's so cold and bare and lonely there, Ted. Why did Father have to sign up with the Martian Archeology Society?"

Ted looked at her with some surprise. "Dad talked this over with us. You said you wanted to go."

"It didn't seem so scary then, although I didn't really *want* to go, but out here in the dark where there's never a sunrise and everything is so still and quiet, I—I feel afraid!"

"Does Dad or Mom know you feel this way?" Ted asked.

She shook her head. "Father's counted so much on us going to Mars. He was so lonely there before without us. If he knew I didn't want to go, he'd feel he had to get a job on Earth. But you know his first love is excavation on Mars."

"You'll be all right, Sis, when we get settled in our new home. They've got it all ready for us. Think of the fun it'll be!" Ted said encouragingly.

Jill seemed to feel better and smiled. Both turned their attention to the wondrous misty veil of the Milky Way outside. It reminded Ted of a great caravan of countless tiny sheep trooping through the endless black of space night. Each one of those millions of light points he knew to be individual giant suns. How frighteningly huge and marvelous was God's universe!

Directly in front of them hung the wrinkled

"The Earth!" She spoke in awe.

gray face of Luna, the Moon, which they would pass before long. Ted shuddered at its forbidding deep pits and miles of barren, dead plains.

Jill leaned forward eagerly on the window seat on which they were perched, her nose almost touching the clear plastic window. "Ted!" she exclaimed. "What's that green ball below us?"

Ted looked, then grinned. "Don't you even know your own planet when you see it?"

"The Earth!" She spoke in awe. "Of course!"

Ted was not surprised that his sister had not recognized the globe, in so far as neither of them had seen it before from this dramatic position. Ever since their fire-off from the Arizona space harbor, the Earth had been out of their view, beneath them.

"Look!" Jill cried. "I can make out the outline of Africa! It looks like it's buried under fog. I didn't know before that you could actually *see* the atmosphere!"

"I knew it," Ted said, with mock superiority. "I bet you don't know it's hundreds of miles deep."

"You're not the only one who knows the answers, Ted Kenton, even if you are pretty smart," she returned. "I know that it's the lack of atmosphere out here in space that makes everything so crystal clear. That's why we can see so many thousands more stars out here than we can from Earth under a layer of air."

"That's not bad for a girl," Ted replied, with a tolerant grin.

She shoved him in playful displeasure. Although the push was not hard, it upset Ted's balance, and he slipped off the window seat and rolled onto the metal floor. Jill gasped in alarm and darted to his side. As she tried to help him up, she too lost her equilibrium and fell beside him. Ted looked at her and laughed.

Their awkwardness was caused by the fact that they wore magnetized shoes that were attracted to the metal floor of the space ship. Even when sitting down, they had kept the soles of their shoes on the metal of the seat. Ted got to his feet and helped Jill up.

"Will we ever get used to these funny shoes?" Jill complained.

"We'll have to," Ted said. "If we didn't wear

them we'd go floating around in the air like a feather. That's another disadvantage of leaving Earth. We don't have any weight at all in space. If we wanted to, we could take off our shoes and stretch out in the air just like on a soft couch."

"It might be fun to swim around in here just like a fish," Jill mused. "I think I'll try it."

Ted knew he should stop her, but his curiosity to see such an experiment prevented him from giving in to the tug of his conscience.

"Be careful!" Ted warned. "Any motion you make will be hard to stop."

When her shoes were off, Jill pressed gently upward from her toes. She shrieked in pleasure as she rose gracefully into the air. Reaching the ceiling of the room, she pushed against it and floated downward again.

"That's lots of fun!" she said. "Why don't you try it, Ted?"

"Uh-uh. Another time. One of us had better keep his feet."

Jill tried other movements, whirling and doing flip-overs. Then she grew bolder, moving more swiftly. She teased Ted into trying to catch her, and he finally got into the game. He lunged at her but missed her fleet form every time. The game grew more active. Presently both of them were scampering about in the space-ship compartment, laughing and having great fun.

Jill paused in one corner beneath an air-vent box. "Try and catch me!" she taunted, her eyes shiny with merriment. "I'll let you get real close."

Ted glided catlike across the floor, his metal-soled shoes clicking at every step. Only when he was nearly upon her did she move. She flexed her knees and soared off above him, laughing. His hands raked the air but missed her agile form.

Suddenly Ted's heart seemed to stop dead. "Jill! Look out! You'll hit that air vent!"

She saw the danger too late. She screamed and crashed heavily into the metal vent, head on. Her head lolled in unconsciousness, and her body hung limp as a broken toy against the ceiling of the space-ship room.

CHAPTER TWO

Hurtling Danger

HIS HEART POUNDING in anxiety at Jill's plight, Ted opened a door and dashed into the next room of the suite.

"Jill!" he cried. "She's hurt!"

Dr. Kenton looked up, startled, from the desk where he had been studying. "Let's go, Son!" the scientist said, jumping to his feet.

"Where's Mom?" Ted asked.

"She's down in the magazine shop," his father answered, and added, "It's probably for the better."

They hurried into the observation room where

17

Ted and Jill had been so happy together only a short time before. The boy pointed overhead at the air vent, where Jill's limp form hung, lighter than a thistle in her weightlessness.

Even Dr. Kenton's tall, stalwart form could not reach high enough to bring her down. "We've got to have something to stand on," he said.

Ted thought of the long window seat. He rushed over and knelt down to examine it. "The window seat is in sections, Dad, and has some clamps holding it down," he said. "We ought to be able to get it loose."

Dr. Kenton's strong fingers released the catches that held the seat in place. Then he lifted it out and carried it across to the spot beneath the air vent. He stood on the seat and grasped Jill's slim body, bringing it down.

The girl was stretched out waist high in the air, in which position her father could best see her injury. Ted held her so that a sudden movement would not send her floating off. The scientist found a cut on Jill's temple where she had struck the air vent. She began stirring. In a few seconds she had recovered consciousness. She was pale and smiled feebly.

"What happened to me?" she asked in a weak voice.

Only then did Dr. Kenton seem concerned about the cause of the accident. He looked inquiringly at Ted. "Well, Ted," he said, "what did happen?"

"She wanted to go without her shoes to see what it felt like," Ted replied. "I should have stopped her."

"You both should be tanned for a trick like that," his father said gravely. "Jill could have been seriously injured."

They helped Jill to the window seat, then put on her magnetic shoes for her. She said she felt all right, but her father insisted that she have the cut treated. A brief visit to the first-aid cabinet, built into the wall of the room, had Jill's hurt taken care of in a few moments.

"What prompted you two to try such a stunt as this?" Dr. Kenton asked as he closed the door of the first-aid cabinet. "I thought you had been well grounded on the facts of weightless bodies in space."

Ted, embarrassed, kicked the seat section they had removed, forgetting that it was not fastened down. It scooted off in the air, but Dr. Kenton alertly grabbed it before it got far. "I guess we were just fidgety for something to do," Ted said.

"I suppose the scenery *is* getting a little monotonous for you," their father replied. "Maybe I can arrange for you to stretch your legs a bit."

"You mean we can tour the ship now?" Jill asked excitedly.

"I think so," Dr. Kenton said, "I believe the confusion that always follows the fire-off is pretty well under control now. I'll ask Commander Grissom about it."

Their father left and was back in a short while. "We can go," he told them. "We'll leave a note for Mom to let her know where we've gone."

He scribbled it off, after getting a slip of paper from a drawer in the wall desk. Then he asked them, "What would you like to see first?"

"The pilots' roost!" Ted said, and Jill nodded

"Hi, folks," he greeted.

in agreement. The three of them clicked along the corridor in their magnetic shoes. Reaching the pilots' roost in the nose of the space ship, Dr. Kenton knocked on the door and was told to enter. Inside, the children found two men in the light green with gold trim of the Space Transport Command, sitting in big roomy seats in front of a large bank of dials and levers. Above the panel was a broad port looking out into space.

One of the pilots appeared to be busy. The unoccupied one spun on his swivel seat and smiled at the Kentons. "Hi, folks," he greeted. "Come on in!"

He introduced himself as Lieutenant Foran and his copilot as Lieutenant Starky, who took a moment from his work to smile a greeting.

"On every trip we make we usually let the passengers come in a few at a time," Lieutenant Foran said, "to look around."

The pilot showed them what each dial on the panel meant. Jill was soon bewildered by it all, but Ted was interested in every gadget and meter. He decided at that moment that he would like nothing better than one day to be a pilot on an interplanetary space liner.

Ted had noticed a huge circular screen built into the middle of the panel, with circles radiating out from the center of it. Suddenly it lighted up, and white spots, or "blips," began popping out on the glass's phosphor coating. Ted saw that the pilots' eyes had flashed swiftly toward the screen.

Lieutenant Starky leaned forward and twisted a dial.

"What's he doing?" Ted asked.

"That's the radarscope," Lieutenant Foran said. "The screen automatically lights up when anything comes directly into our path, even if it's many thousands of miles away. Those blips are echoes we're receiving from our approaching neighbors out there."

Lieutenant Foran went over to the panel, looking up at the screen. "What is it?" he asked his companion.

"Seems to be a ship," replied Lieutenant Starky. "Probably the mail rocket *Moonstone* on its way back from Luna. The navigator said we'd pass it."

Lieutenant Foran slid into his seat and pressed a button on the panel. A voice from a speaker said, "Navigation."

The young Kentons heard the two crewmen speak in low tones for several moments. Then Lieutenant Foran switched off and turned to the copilot with an apprehensive look on his face. "He says the *Moonstone* should have turned off course before now! It's heading straight toward us!"

"We'll call the Commander!" Lieutenant Starky said, jabbing a button.

Jill squeezed her father's arm. "Are we going to crash?" she whispered.

"Don't be scared, honey," her father said soothingly. "I'm sure we'll be all right."

But Ted saw the fear in his dad's eyes, and his own heart seemed to squirm with terror in his body. Was their very first journey into space going to end tragically scarcely before it had started?

CHAPTER THREE

First Stop—Luna

I CAN'T UNDERSTAND why they don't turn off course!" Lieutenant Starky exclaimed. "Their radar *must* have contacted us!"

Ted watched the blips from the *Moonstone* slowly nearing the center of the screen. By the time they did reach that center, the *Moonstone* and the *Shooting Star* would be occupying the same area in space.

Lieutenant Foran came over to the Kentons. "I think you folks had better get back to your suite. We're going to be awfully busy in here for the next few minutes," he said.

Ted could see that the officer was trying to

keep the fear out of his voice. They must really be in a bad spot.

As they left, they met stout, red-faced Commander Grissom coming in. His face was redder than usual, and he was so concerned with the *Shooting Star's* danger that he barely nodded to Dr. Kenton.

As the Kentons returned to their quarters, golden-haired Mrs. Kenton faced her family with stricken eyes.

"What's happening, John?" she asked her husband. "All the crewmen are running around like mad."

"It's just a little trouble outside," the scientist said gently. "I'm sure Commander Grissom and his men can handle it."

Mrs. Kenton began pacing restlessly. "This waiting! I wish we knew what's going on."

"We can," the scientist said, crossing the room and pressing a button on a wall panel. "I thought it might upset us more to listen in, but I guess it would be better to know what they're doing."

They heard first the voice of Lieutenant Starky

coming over the compartment's loud-speaker. *"The Moonstone* has just answered, sir!"

"What do they say?" the commander asked urgently.

After a few moments' pause, the Kentons heard the pilot speak again: "They say that they had some electronic trouble and that it's just now been repaired. Their radio and radar were off because of it."

Ted listened tensely as orders flew back and forth. Both space ships set their rocket jets to carry each away from the other, but at the speeds they were traveling, only time would tell if they could avoid a crash.

The Kentons heard the final miles being slowly called off by Commander Grissom as the two ships hurtled toward one another:

"Four hundred—three hundred—two—a hundred and fifty. . . ."

Ted's eyes were on the side port. He knew that at the last moment either he would see a large silver shape hurtle past the window or he would feel the might of tons crashing head on. In the final seconds, Dr. Kenton had an arm around his

27

wife and daughter, and Ted's heart was thumping wildly.

The light of thousands of stars out there seemed to burn into the boy's brain. Would the decisive moment never come?

Presently Ted saw the blackness of space blurred for only the briefest instant as the *Moonstone* drove past, its rockets streaming tongues of flame! The side jets spurted against the hull of the *Shooting Star,* causing it to rock. Ted felt the floor tilting beneath him, and he had to grab a wall rail for support. A glimpse he caught of his parents and Jill showed that they were having the same trouble.

As the ship steadied itself and drove on an even keel again, Ted grinned weakly. "We—we made it," he managed to say.

The faces of Jill and her mother were still chalky with fright, but Dr. Kenton's was as calm as if he had known the *Shooting Star* would come through the peril all right.

They heard the voice of Commander Grissom over the speaker informing the passengers that the danger was past. Dr. Kenton then cut off the speaker.

"I never want to go through an experience like that again!" cried Mrs. Kenton, taking a seat.

"I don't think we need ever fear this happening again," Dr. Kenton said. "It's quite a rare occurrence."

"What about meteors?" Jill asked.

"They're rare too, fortunately," he answered. "I don't see why we can't expect an uneventful trip from now until we reach our home on Mars."

Hearing this confident remark, the children were interested in the space ship again. "We didn't finish our tour!" Jill burst out.

"Would you like to see the garden?" Dr. Kenton asked.

"The garden?" Ted asked, puzzled. "What good is a garden on a space ship?"

"Come along and you'll see," Dr. Kenton said and started for the door. Mrs. Kenton said she preferred to stay in the suite and collect her shattered nerves, but the children, of course, were eager to go.

"Haven't you two wondered how you're able to breathe in the ship?" their father asked as they walked down the corridor.

"I know how," Ted said. "The air is pumped

through the ship from compressed-air chambers."

"What is air?" his father asked.

"Mostly oxygen and nitrogen," Ted answered.

"The *Shooting Star* uses oxygen, with helium instead of nitrogen to dilute it," Dr. Kenton said. "That's so that, in case a meteor penetrates the ship, the rapid decompression won't cause us to get bubbles in our blood, which is a dangerous condition called 'the Bends.'"

"But what's that to do with a garden?" Jill asked.

"You'll see in a minute," came the reply.

An attendant showed them through the "garden." There was not much to see. There were merely rows and rows of broad-leaved plants covered with plastic and a network of tubes.

"Some garden," Ted murmured, when the attendant had walked off to answer a call. "The plants aren't pretty and they don't seem to have fruit or vegetables either."

"They yield something even more precious, though," his father said. "Oxygen."

"Huh?" Ted asked in surprise.

31

Dr. Kenton smiled at the puzzled looks on their faces. "Plants and people are well suited to one another," he said. "Plants breathe out oxygen into our Earth's atmosphere, and in gratitude we give them back carbon dioxide which, as you know, we breathe out."

"So that's it!" Jill said.

"It's really quite simple," the scientist went on. "These plants keep our oxygen tanks filled, and the air exhaled by us is pumped back to them so that they can keep alive."

"Will our home on Mars have a garden producing air?" Ted asked.

"No, we'll use air cartridges there because they're more efficient in small places."

Just then the attendant returned. "The commander has ordered all passengers back to their suites to prepare for emergency landing," he told them. "Jet fire from the *Moonstone* damaged our hull, and we've got to lay over on Luna for repairs."

"Goody!" Jill exclaimed. "We'll get to land on the Moon!"

They returned to the main compartment of

their suite, and Dr. Kenton switched on the wall speaker so that he could hear the order from the commander to "strap down."

As they waited, they stood before the big window looking out on the rugged globe of Luna. Dr. Kenton pressed a button on the sill that slid a darkening filter over the window. In this way, the blinding glare of the full moon was cut down considerably.

"Those big craters look just like eyes!" Ted exclaimed.

"It's all so terribly rough-looking down there, I don't see where we can land!" Mrs. Kenton said.

The scientist pointed. "See that large gray plain down there?" he said. "It's the Sea of Serenity, and the Moon colony is located on one edge of it. We're too far away yet to see it."

"Hey, we're turning around!" Ted exclaimed, as he saw the stars beginning to blur before his eyes.

"That's so that we can use our rear jets to brake our landing," the scientist said.

The order to pull down couches and "strap

down" came over the speaker a few minutes later. Each of the Kentons opened a door in the wall and pulled down his foam-rubber cot. The couches were fastened securely to the floor with catches. The family stretched out on the soft mattresses. They pulled up the plastic straps from the sides and tightened them across their bodies.

Presently a crewman stuck his head in the door to make sure they were ready for the strain of landing.

Some time later, when he had the sensation of going down in a suddenly dropping elevator, Ted knew the moment of deceleration had begun.

In his mind's eye he could picture what was going on. He imagined the long sleekness of the *Shooting Star* plunging toward the moon's rough surface. From the ship's rocket tubes, streams of fire were pouring out to slow the terrific speed of the ship. If those fire streams should fail, or not hold back the craft enough, the rocket would be dashed to bits on Luna.

As the ship slackened its speed, Ted felt steadily worse. It was as if his chest were being crushed. He knew that he and the others could stand any top speed the rocket would go; that it was only a change in speed that was so grueling.

He twisted his head and saw the other members of his family buried deeply in their couches. He knew they were suffering as badly as he. He remembered the danger of the *Shooting Star* and *Moonstone* approaching one another in the heavens. Then he thought what a frightful crash it would have been had they met.

It made him wonder, now, if the *Shooting Star* could check its downward plunge in time, or if it would be dashed to atoms on the hard gray soil of Luna.

CHAPTER FOUR

The Curious Boy

J UST AS Ted was expecting the worst, he felt a
gentle bump beneath him. He looked around
and saw that the rest of his family were no longer
deep in their couches. That meant the heavy
pressure of their descent was off them. They must
have already landed!

But he could not get up yet, for he was in a
vertical position and hanging by his straps. This
was because the rocket had landed upright on its
tail fins.

Ted heard a rumbling sound. He felt the side
of the room to which the couches were fastened
slide down into normal position. Ted unbuckled
his straps and rose to his feet.

37

"Hey, it's time to get up!" he said to the others.

Dr. Kenton unstrapped himself and then assisted Mrs. Kenton. Ted helped get Jill loose.

"Whew! That was awful!" Mrs. Kenton complained.

"I—I think I left my stomach up in the sky!" Jill said.

Ted started toward the side window. "I feel so heavy!" he said. "I can hardly lift my feet!"

His father plodded with him to the window. "That's because the gravity of Luna is added to the ship's artificial gravity. They'll cut off the rocket gravity any moment."

Looking out the window, Ted thought that this was like a scene from a fairy tale. Any moment he expected to see a group of gnomes come frolicking past! But nothing appeared to be alive in that craggy, lonely wilderness, except within the man-made structure of lunar rock.

Jill and her mother, having taken longer to get their bearings, finally joined the other two at the window.

"What makes it so awfully bright out there?" asked Jill, squinting her eyes.

"Don't forget that we have a blanket of atmosphere to protect us from the sun on earth, but here on Luna the sun strikes with full force," her father explained.

"Talk about a sunburn!" Ted said, with a whistle.

"You couldn't stand it long," Dr. Kenton said, chuckling grimly. "It's hot enough to boil water out there right now!"

"Then when the sun is down, it must be nice," put in Mrs. Kenton innocently.

Her husband grinned. "If you call over two hundred degrees below zero centigrade nice!"

A crisp voice came over the speaker: "All passengers to the dressing room to don space gear!"

"You mean we have to go out in that?" Mrs. Kenton asked, shocked.

"I don't know any other way of getting to the settlement across the way," was Dr. Kenton's gentle reply.

As the Kentons were walking along the corri-

39

dor to the dressing room, they suddenly felt light on their feet. The unexpectedness of it sent them colliding with one another. A voice from a wall speaker said: "Watch your step. The artificial gravity of the ship has been cut off."

"I feel like a feather!" Jill said, dancing along.

"You should—you weigh only one sixth of your Earth weight," her father said. "But you be careful or you'll have another accident like you did earlier!"

The passengers lined up to receive their space gear. It was bulky equipment, but not very heavy in the light gravity. In the dressing room, several crewmen demonstrated how to put on the space suits.

Dr. Kenton, who had put on much space gear in his time, helped his family into theirs.

"Climb into the flexible suit first," he said, as he demonstrated. "Then all you have to do is to zip it up—so!"

"What are these tubes on our backs?" Jill asked, after the asbestos-covered suits were donned.

"That's your oxygen source," her father said.

"Those smaller boxes are refrigerator units that cool the air so that you won't burn up in the terrible heat out there."

Weighted shoes were pulled on next. These were heavy, in order to bring the wearer more nearly to his Earth weight. Dr. Kenton helped them on next with their plastic fish-bowl helmets, fastening them in place with catches.

They found that they could talk to one another, even from the air-tight helmets, because of a compact radio attachment on the top. Last to be put on were protective gloves.

When everyone in the dressing room was fully attired, the strange company left the ship through an air lock—a pair of doors which kept the air pressure from escaping. The *Shooting Star's* gangplank, which was actually a long escalator, slid out of the side of the ship on gears until the bottom touched ground. Then the passengers stepped out of the air lock onto it and were carried slowly downward. The rocket, in landing on her tail fins, was now in position for the fire-off later into space.

"What a strange feeling it is," thought Ted,

setting foot on a world outside of his own beloved Earth! The ground they walked on was soft and powdery, and his father said it was called pumice.

The party was heading for a ring of stone buildings ahead, which were connected to one another by long tunnels. It reminded Ted of a giant wheel turned over on the ground. At the center was the largest building of all. Ted asked his father what it was.

"That's the headquarters building," the scientist answered. "It's called the Hub, and it acts as a central control for all the other buildings around the circle."

"Why are the buildings connected with one another?" Jill wanted to know.

"That's so the people inside can go from one to the other without having to put on space suits. You see, all the buildings and connecting corridors are filled with compressed air. The Moon has no air of its own, so it has to be manufactured just as it is on the *Shooting Star*."

Ted thought his father's voice sounded queer coming over his helmet receiver, but he guessed he would get used to it in time.

"That's the headquarters building."

The party from the *Shooting Star* entered a building where they removed their space suits. They were told that they were free to do whatever they liked until the ship was repaired for the journey to Mars.

Some of the passengers said that they would like to make a tour of the Wheel, and when others also expressed a wish to do so, a guide took the entire party around. The Kenton children found that most of the departments had to do with scientific research, while the rest were devoted to the running of the colony.

"Did they haul all these stones from Earth to build this place?" Ted asked, as they went down one of the long rock passageways.

"Goodness no!" his father replied with a laugh. "The whole colony is built of lunar rock, quarried near by."

When the Wheel had been circled by the sightseers and it was learned that the *Shooting Star* would not be ready for hours for the fire-off, Dr. Kenton made a suggestion to his family as they sat idly with the other passengers in the lounge.

"I have an astronomer friend who runs an observatory not far from here," he said. "Would you kids like to visit it?"

Their eyes sparkled with enthusiasm, and they both nodded as one. Mrs. Kenton, however, was not so ambitious.

"Not I," she sighed. "That long walk around this building will last me for a good while."

Ted noticed a sandy-haired boy of his own age watching them closely. Even as they made the tour around the Wheel, the boy had listened intently to everything Dr. Kenton had said. And when the scientist had mentioned going to Mars, Ted saw that his eyes had lighted up as though with longing.

"We won't be able to take the other passengers with us," Dr. Kenton told his son and daughter, "because there aren't enough cars available."

After Dr. Kenton had chartered a car from the motor pool, he and his son and daughter went to the dressing room to climb into their space gear. As they were zipping up their suits, Ted looked toward the open doorway and saw the same curious boy watching them again! What could be his interest in them?

CHAPTER FIVE

Pelting Stones

TED DECIDED he would find out just why the boy was watching them. "Hello," Ted greeted.

"Hi," the boy answered.

"What's your name?" Ted asked.

"Randy Matthews," the boy returned.

Before Ted could go on with his questioning, Dr. Kenton spoke up. "Randy, would you like to go with us to visit the observatory?"

"Yes, sir, I would," was the ready reply.

"You'd better check with your folks first," Dr. Kenton advised.

"I don't have any folks here," Randy said.

47

"Mr. Collins is taking care of me. He's an engineer."

"Then check with him and come on back if you can," Dr. Kenton said.

When Randy had left, Ted said, "He's been watching us a long time, Dad, just as if he couldn't wait to make friends with us."

"I've noticed it, too," his father said. "I wonder what he meant when he said he has no folks *here?*"

Randy got back shortly and said he could go with them. The Kentons had to wait for him to dress, but they were surprised at his speed. He seemed to know all the fasteners and fittings perfectly.

The four of them left the building and went outside where an odd vehicle awaited them.

"What a funny-looking car!" Jill exclaimed, and Ted could hear her merry laugh ring in his helmet receiver.

"A fresh-air taxi!" Ted put in.

The car had enormous tires and an open top. It looked more like a tractor than anything else.

"Let's climb in," Dr. Kenton said. He helped

the children in, then took the driver's seat. He turned a switch, and they were off.

When they had gotten up speed, Ted thought this the most exciting ride he had ever taken! They bounced along over the rough ground without feeling any of the bumps. Dr. Kenton explained that the tires were low-pressured and shock-absorbent.

The young folks were so impressed by their ride that it was much later before they took time to notice the breath-taking beauty of the sky. The stars were so numerous, they looked like swaths of white dust against the absolute blackness. Randy was the first to notice the big green globe of Earth behind them, and pointed it out.

"It makes me homesick seeing it," Jill said, and Ted detected a tremor in her voice.

Ted couldn't help admiring Jill for her courage in agreeing to come along against her wishes, just to keep the family together.

When the Moon car reached the observatory, Ted did not find exactly what he had expected. Instead of a white tower, like the observatories at home, what he saw was a natural, tall column of jagged rock, on the top of which was a man-made shiny dome with a slit in it where the telescope eye peeped out.

The four got out of the car and walked through a doorway that had been blasted through the rock in some time past. Beyond this was an air lock that kept the compressed air of the observatory from escaping.

When they had gone through the door, the four found facing them a crude elevator. Dr. Kenton motioned the young people inside and then followed. He threw a switch, and the elevator cage began rising slowly.

"This column of rock has always been hollow," he explained, "so it was easy to run an elevator up through it."

He unfastened his helmet and took it off. "You can take off your hats now," he told the children. "There's air in here."

The elevator stopped at the top of the shaft. The four got out and entered a big room with a rounded ceiling. Ted knew this to be the dome that housed the telescope. The reflector was like a huge cylinder resting in its horseshoe yoke across the room.

"Hello!" Dr. Kenton called. "Is anyone home?"

Suddenly a round face appeared at the side of

the telescope. The face reminded Ted of a circus clown's, with its wild, wispy hair and broad grin.

"John Kenton!" cried the little man, as he ran out and embraced Ted's dad. The elderly scientist asked, "What in the world are you doing on Luna? And who are these young folks with you?"

Dr. Kenton explained that he was on a stopover to Mars, and he introduced the children to the funny little scientist, whose name was Dr. Beeler.

"We had some time to kill so we decided to visit the observatory," Dr. Kenton finished. "Will you show the children some of the sights?"

Dr. Beeler's eyes brightened with pleasure. Ted was sure that the little man was truly enjoying their visit. Ted thought he must get awfully lonesome up here by himself.

Dr. Beeler set the position of the telescope by turning two cranks. Then he conducted the children up a catwalk to a platform about twelve feet from the floor. Jill took the first peek through the eyepiece at the top of the tube.

"Oooh—it's beautiful!" Jill cried with a gasp.

Ted let Randy have the next turn, and then he himself looked. The view was breath-taking. What he saw was the flattened, white globe of Saturn with its graceful rings and many satellites.

"The Moon is much better than the Earth for using a telescope," Dr. Beeler said, "because here there is no atmosphere or haze to get in the way."

The children saw other captivating sights.

There was the shimmering pearl of Venus, Earth's twin, then Jupiter, the king of planets, with its four orderly larger moons. The children also saw smoky-looking nebulae and star clusters that resembled bees in a hive. Then Dr. Beeler showed them what he seemed to think was the greatest treat of all—the Earth under high magnification. When Jill placed her eye to the eyepiece, she suddenly turned away, sobbing.

Dr. Beeler and her father came running to her.

"What's the matter, honey?" Dr. Kenton asked.

"I—I guess I'm homesick!" Jill said. I miss the green grass and the blue sky terribly! Oh, why did we ever have to leave home?"

Ted saw his father's face grow grave. Now his dad knew that Jill had never wanted to come along. Her father placed his arm around her shoulders. "I didn't know you felt this way," he said softly.

Dr. Beeler stood by, fidgeting as though he wanted to say something but didn't know just what.

Presently Dr. Kenton looked at his wrist watch

which he could read through the plastic cuff of his space suit. "We'd better get back to the colony," he said. The *Shooting Star* may be nearly ready to take off."

They came down off the catwalk to the floor level where they took their leave of Dr. Beeler. Ted saw a sad look in the old astronomer's eyes as though he would have liked them to stay longer.

"Good luck to all of you," Dr. Beeler said. Then to Jill he added, "Don't worry, young lady. You won't find Mars such a bad place. And you'll be seeing the good old Earth again, some day, too."

As the four went down in the elevator, Jill said, "I'm sorry I was such a baby."

"Nonsense," her father returned. "I must confess I've been a little homesick myself since leaving Earth. How about you,' Ted, and you, Randy?"

Ted had to admit to a certain amount himself, but the Kentons were surprised to hear Randy's opinion.

"No sir," Randy said, "I'm not homesick for Earth."

Ted could not understand why a person should prefer the other planets to their own home world. Ted could see that his father felt the same, for he gave their new young friend an odd look.

Ted thought it would be a good time to learn something more about the mysterious Randy, and he was about to ask some questions when the cage touched the ground floor.

"Everybody out," Dr. Kenton said. "Put on your helmets and turn on your air valves."

There was no time for questioning now. The three younger folks did as instructed. Ted liked the caressing feeling he got as the air pumped up his suit. It was like a soft summer breeze against his skin. It made him want to giggle.

The explorers climbed into their car outside, and Dr. Kenton started it. Then they went flying across the bleak gray moonscape, back toward the Wheel. Jill had gotten over her gloom, and the excitement of the carefree ride prompted her to start singing. It was a well-known song that all the school children at home knew, and Ted and her father both joined in. Dr. Kenton invited Randy to chime in, but the boy surprised them once more when he said that he did not even know the song! This only added to the mystery of Randy.

Suddenly the scientist jammed the brakes on so suddenly that the children were pitched forward.

"What's wrong?" Ted asked, when he had regained his wits.

He was surprised to see his father leap from his seat and vault to the ground. "Out of here—all of you—quickly!" he urged.

His insistent voice brought them tumbling out of the car to the ground.

"What is it?" Jill cried frantically.

"See those spurts of dust just up ahead?" her father said, pointing. "They're meteorites striking the ground. We almost blundered right into a meteor shower!"

He looked around. "We've got to find some

shelter," he told them. "A cave—a clump of rocks
—anything."

"There's a bunch of rocks!" Randy said, indicating a clump off to their left.

"That seems to be the closest place!" Dr. Kenton said. "Let's go!"

They broke into a run across the ground, slipping and sliding in the powdery pumice. Ted saw bursts of Moon dust closer now, and they were coming with greater frequency. One huge geyser several feet away threw a shower of sand over all of them, blinding them momentarily.

When the "air" cleared, Ted was shocked to find Randy missing.

"Where's Randy?" he cried.

"There he is—on the ground," Jill shrieked, pointing behind them.

Ted turned, and his heart seemed to stop beating for a moment. Randy was stretched out flat. He was unmoving, still as death!

CHAPTER SIX

Into Space Again

THE KENTONS dashed out into the open to the spot where their young friend lay. They bent over him. He was struggling feebly, and his mouth was open and gasping as though he could not get his breath. His suit was almost deflated. The meteorites had stopped falling, and there was no further danger from them.

Ted saw that his father seemed to know just what to do. He swiftly zipped open a pocket in the side of Randy's suit and took out a small strip of sticky fabric. There was a tiny slit in the boy's suit where a stone had grazed it. Dr. Kenton stuck the strip over the tear and pressed it firmly.

Then he opened wider the air valve on Randy's helmet, and the suit puffed out again.

Presently Randy's eyes opened, and he pushed himself up into a sitting position.

"What happened?" he asked, almost in a whisper.

"A meteorite grazed your suit, deflating it," the scientist replied. "For a few seconds you were like a fish out of water. We'll have the doctor check you over when we get back, but I think we brought you around in time."

They helped him to his feet. At first, he was wobbly, but he soon regained his full strength and was able to walk alone by the time they reached the car.

They climbed into the Moon vehicle and went whirling off in another swift-paced ride back toward the Wheel. When they arrived at the Moon colony, Dr. Kenton had a physician examine Randy to make sure he was all right, which proved to be the case.

Soon the broadcasting loud-speakers announced that the *Shooting Star* had been repaired and would fire off within the next hour.

In the waiting room the Kentons held what they believed was their last meeting with their new friend Randy.

There was still much about the boy which puzzled Ted—there were loads of questions he would have liked to ask him. Although he did not talk much, Randy seemed to like to be with the Kentons. And now that the parting was nearly at hand, Ted thought he appeared very downcast.

"We'll sure miss you, Randy," Jill was saying.

"Yes, we will," Mrs. Kenton said kindly. "Too bad you can't go along with us."

At this last remark, Randy looked up wistfully. Ted had an idea that Randy would like nothing better than to go with them.

"Have you ever been to Mars, Randy?" Ted asked.

"Of course," he replied gently. "I was born there."

All the Kentons straightened in surprise. No wonder Randy had said he was not homesick for Earth, Ted thought. He knew the boy did not mean that he was a native Martian, but that his father was an Earthman who had been on Mars when Randy had been born.

Ted knew that his father had decided to evade the mystery of Randy no longer when he asked the direct question: "Randy, do you mind telling us where your parents are?"

Randy's eyes dropped, and his slender fingers began twisting.

"My mother is dead. My father is somewhere on Mars with an engineering expedition. That's why Mr. Collins is taking care of me. He's a close friend of Father's."

"Son, do you know which expedition your father is with?" Dr. Kenton asked.

"Yes, sir," Randy answered. "It's the Number Five Syrtis Major Expedition."

Ted was watching his father as he asked the question. A cold, unexplainable feeling coursed through him. When Randy replied, Dr. Kenton's face suddenly paled, and he turned away. Ted felt a stab of dread. Had something happened to the No. 5 Expedition? What a terrible tragedy for Randy if this were so.

"I sure miss Pops," Randy said softly, a

dreamy look on his face. "I haven't seen him for two years. We had lots of fun together. He was teaching me to play baseball—helping me develop a curve."

This was the most Randy had ever said at one time, and the Kentons listened raptly. Ted could see that his father was disturbed over Randy's case. He took out his handkerchief and blew his nose hard.

"Randy, how would you like to go to Mars with us?" Dr. Kenton asked presently.

Ted saw the sunshine of joy flare up in the boy's face. "C—could I?" he asked. "Really?"

"Of course," the scientist said. "We'd be glad to have you, wouldn't we, Mom?"

Mrs. Kenton smiled softly at the boy. "We certainly would, Randy."

Randy needed no further urging. First he checked with his guardian, Mr. Collins, who came to see Dr. Kenton. Mr. Collins was a husky, friendly person. Randy was off packing as the men talked in the presence of the other Kentons.

"I think it would be the best thing in the world for the boy," Mr. Collins said thoughtfully. "The Fifth Expedition was given up for lost about a week ago. I've kept it from Randy all this time, hoping that the lost explorers would turn up. But they never have."

"I knew about the expedition," Ted's father said. "That's why I want to take him. I thought we'd accept him into our family, so that when the news came to him, he might not take it so hard. I guess I've got a soft spot in my heart for the pioneers on Mars, being a scientist myself."

"It's a grand thing you're doing," Mr. Collins said.

When Mr. Collins left, Mrs. Kenton said to her husband, "We'll have to tell Randy about his father ourselves, won't we?"

"In due time," Dr. Kenton replied, "after he comes to know us better. It'll be easier that way."

"Randy will be able to tell us all about Mars, since he's from there," Jill said excitedly.

Ted agreed with his sister and decided then that Randy was going to make a very welcome addition to the Kenton household.

Less than an hour later, the *Shooting Star* was in the heavens again, powering toward the dis-

He was going to Mars.

tant red beacon of Mars and leaving behind the rugged wastelands of the Moon.

Randy became a much more chipper person than the silent boy the Kentons had first met. New life seemed to have flowed into him. He was going to Mars, the land of his birth and the place where he believed his beloved father to be—alive. Ted felt sorry for the boy in the days that followed, whenever he talked about the good times he and his father had had together. When the time came to tell him about his father, it was not going to be an easy job for Ted's dad.

In the eternal night of interplanetary space, time seemed to stand still. Ted knew that days and days, even weeks, had passed since leaving the Moon, but without the rising and setting of a sun to go by, it hardly seemed that any time had passed at all.

By now the Moon had lost its roundness and had become just another star in the sky. The red spark of Mars, however, was growing day after day, week after week. However, it could not yet be recognized as a disk.

One day Ted noticed what looked like a

smudge across the blackness of the sky. It blotted out the stars behind it and appeared to be close. But its movement was scarcely noticeable. Ted called his father's attention to the blur of light.

"It looks like a comet!" Dr. Kenton said. "I'll check with the commander."

The scientist tuned in a two-way speaker system and asked about Ted's find.

"That's Brooking's Comet, discovered back in 1970," Commander Grissom replied. "It circles the sun every eight years. You're in for a treat. We'll pass through some of its vapor. It'll be a spectacular sight a few days from now."

Watching the comet took up nearly all of the idle time of Ted, Jill, and Randy in the hours that followed. Under Dr. Kenton's guidance they drew a chart of that part of the sky in which it was located, and plotted its motion in relation to that of the space ship.

"You don't suppose it'll crash into us, do you?" Mrs. Kenton asked worriedly, as the comet loomed menacingly outside their compartment window some time later.

Dr. Kenton soothed her with a smile. "Don't

67

worry," he said. "If the skipper says we'll graze it, that's exactly what will happen. He knows every inch of this comet's orbit and our own too!"

Dr. Kenton explained that the comet appeared to move slowly because it was coming practically head on. Steadily it blossomed wider, like an opening flower bud. In the center was a brilliant light, which was the head, or nucleus.

"Why won't the gravitation of the comet pull us into it?" Ted asked.

"That's because a comet has very little mass, or what we'd call real body, to it. It's mostly a big lump of widely scattered gas particles."

"How big is it?" Jill asked.

"The head is almost as big as Luna, and it has a tail many thousands of miles long," her father answered. "It'll pass us at hundreds of miles a second, but it will take a long time to get by and will hardly seem to be moving."

When the day of the arrival of the comet's nucleus came, every eye on the *Shooting Star* was peering intently out the windows of the rocket ship. The commander had ordered all windows covered with filter screens to cut out the blinding glare of the nucleus.

The comet arrived with the shocking brilliance of a gigantic fireball. All Ted could see was an over-all blinding whiteness that made the blackness of space like bright noonday. The stars were blotted out completely in the glare. For hours the brilliance continued without letup, and then it began to dim.

"The head is past," Dr. Kenton said. "From now on, the light will grow weaker and weaker as the tail goes by."

Ted still could make out no detail of any kind, and this was disappointing. As he and Jill and Randy kept their eyes glued to the window, all they could see was a slow dimming of the comet's original brilliance. They grew weary of the sight and turned away from it. When they returned to it many hours later, the heavens had a strange bluish cast, and the stars began to burn through it weakly.

Still later, only the barest evidence of the celestial body remained. The heavens were only slightly grayed, showing that the tip of the tail alone had not passed.

"Will we see the comet after it swings around the sun, and heads out into space again?" Ted asked.

"Yes, from a greater distance," his father answered. "Then it will look more like a comet to you."

Several days later, Jill came running into their compartment, looking concerned. "Father, I saw some of the passengers going forward into the pilots' roost. They stayed there a few minutes, then came out, and some more people went in. What do you suppose it's all about?"

"I have an idea the commander has a treat for us," her father replied with a knowing grin. "We'll get our turn. Just wait."

Their chance came shortly later. The Kentons and Randy were summoned forward, and they entered the pilots' roost.

"Want to see something?" the commander asked. "Look out the forward window."

They spoke first to the pilots they had met before, then peered out the window. Ted's breath came fast. Poised regally against the backdrop of stars was a gleaming red-orange globe. It was the planet Mars, their new home.

Invisible Menace

THE KENTONS studied the red planet in silent
awe. Beneath the thin cotton of atmosphere,
they saw the crisscross markings of the canals that
had baffled Earthmen for many years. Two small
globes hovered in the deeps beyond. They were
the two moons, Phobos and Deimos.

Randy unconsciously shoved forward ahead of
the Kentons. "Isn't it beautiful!" he murmured.

"I wonder when we'll be landing," Jill said.

The commander, who had heard her, answered, "In fifty hours, young lady."

"I guess we'd better get back to our suite so
that some of the other passengers can come in,"
Dr. Kenton said.

They thanked the commander and left the pilots' roost. When they had returned to their compartment, Ted asked Randy, "Have you ever been to Earth?"

Randy shook his head. "It sounds like a terrific place, though. I've studied a lot about it in our Earth Geography course in school, and Pops has told me a lot about it. Imagine playing baseball outdoors without a space suit on!"

Ted realized he had always taken the wonders of Earth for granted. It was hard to understand that a boy such as Randy existed—a boy who had never experienced such a free life. He tried to imagine how it would be if he had lived all of his life on a world where all the breaths you took were from tanks of artificial air, and where you could never feel the cooling breezes of summer or the spicy winter winds in your lungs. Thinking about these things made Ted thankful that he was not in Randy's shoes.

Suddenly an urgent voice came over the speaker in the Kentons' suite: "Attention, everyone. Act quickly but do not be frightened. A leak has developed in our antiradiation shield.

Everyone retire immediately to the rear store compartment at the extreme end of the ship."

"My goodness!" exclaimed Mrs. Kenton. "What does that mean?"

"There'll be time for explanations later," replied Dr. Kenton. "The first thing is to do as he says."

They hurried out of the compartment and down the corridor aft. There were crewmen stationed along the aisle at intervals to calm the people's fears and keep them orderly. A warning bell signifying trouble was pealing throughout the ship.

The Kentons and Randy crowded into the farthest rear room of the *Shooting Star* with the other passengers, all of whom were chattering excitedly. When the last passenger was in, the transparent door was fastened shut.

"Why did we have to come way back here, Father?" Jill asked.

"Because rays are loose in the ship," her father replied. "The farther we are from the atomic engines up front, the safer we are."

"Are they dangerous?" his wife asked.

"They could be, in sufficient intensity. Right now, they're closing all the doors along the corridors. The doors have built-in screens to resist the rays, if they are not too strong. Keep your eyes on the light bulb out in the corridor. If it turns red, it means the rays have penetrated that far!"

"Oh, dear!" groaned Mrs. Kenton. "I knew we shouldn't have left Earth. Now it looks like we'll never reach our new home, after getting so close, too!"

"Don't worry," Dr. Kenton said. "The ship's crew knows how to handle this. They have electronic instruments they turn on that attract the rays like a magnet. They can clean out the entire ship in about half an hour. That bulb in the corridor will light if even the slightest bit of radiation is present. There's another bulb in the corner of this room, but let's certainly hope this one doesn't light up."

Ted heard a groan from one of the passengers. The light in the corridor was beginning to glow. That meant the radiation had penetrated all the way to the rear of the ship. The next thing to watch was the bulb inside the room, Ted thought. His father had not said so, but Ted guessed that they would probably be in serious trouble if this last one should light.

Presently figures clothed in weird metallic suits and carrying shiny instruments were seen in the corridor.

"The crew is protected by those suits," Dr. Kenton explained. "The things they are carrying are the magnetic ray catchers I was telling you about."

"Look!" Jill said suddenly. "The red light has gone out!"

"We've nothing to worry about, then." The scientist spoke with relief. "I would say those men got to us just in time."

One of the curiously garbed men unfastened the door of the storeroom and beckoned for the passengers to come out. Then he opened the front piece of his helmet to speak to them: "Don't go through the next door until you hear the all-clear whistle," he said. "It'll be just a few minutes."

Figures in weird metallic suits.

When the whistle blew, the corridor doors were opened and the passengers returned to their sections. After the Kentons were back in their suite, Mrs. Kenton sighed deeply and slumped in an air-cushioned chair.

"My goodness!" she said. "I'm still quivery. If it's not one thing it's another on these space voyages! I'm surprised we're still alive after all that's happened!"

"At least you can't say the trip is boring, Mother," Jill piped up, and this brought a relaxing laugh from the others.

Nearly two days later Mars was a giant world dead ahead. Ted looked out the window with Jill and Randy and saw a close-up view of the strange land that was to be their new home. A great network of deep, straight gorges split the boundless stretches of red desert. These were the fabulous canals built by the ancient Martians, now long dead.

"There's the Prime Canal," Randy said, pointing to the largest chasm of all. "It feeds all the little canals in this section."

"Aren't those trees growing along the canals?" Jill asked.

Randy nodded. "Evergreens," he said.

"What's that white stuff in the bottom of the canals and near the roots of the trees?" Ted wanted to know.

"That's frost," Randy answered. "The sun never melts it completely. It never even gets up to zero in this latitude."

Dr. Kenton, whose interest was beyond Mars at the moment, said, "Look, kids, there's our comet again!"

He pointed it out to them in the heavens. It was a long streak across the sky. The nucleus burned brightly, like a heavenly torch.

"Now it really looks like a comet!" Ted declared.

"It's beautiful!" Jill murmured.

"We'll be able to see it from Mars for several days," Dr. Kenton told them. "Then it'll gradually disappear from view."

At this point the *Shooting Star* began its turnabout for rearward landing. Then, still later, the order that all those aboard the *Shooting Star* had been waiting a long time to hear came over the loud-speakers. "Strap down on couches, everyone! Next stop—Lowell Harbor!"

The end of their journey was at hand.

CHAPTER EIGHT

The New World

THE KENTONS had experienced their last landing for a while. After a final gentle bump, Ted shook his head to clear it and waited for the side wall to move into proper position. Then he began unfastening the straps of his couch. He was the first to his feet. As the rest of his family were unbuckling, he did what everyone always did after a space-ship landing. He went over to the window and looked out.

Mars—their new home. At last they were here. From his height of several hundred feet above the ground, Ted had the best view he would ever have of Lowell Harbor, center of Earthmen's activity on the ruddy planet. It had been named in honor of Percival Lowell, the great astronomer of the past century who had been so strongly interested in Martian geography.

Ted felt a breath on his cheek. He turned, and there was Randy right behind him. There were tears of joy in his eyes, and Ted knew that this must be one of the happiest days of Randy's life.

"What a beautiful spaceport!" said Mrs. Kenton, who had come over to the window with the other members of the family.

A huge waterway cut the landscape in two at the edge of the spaceport. Beyond this stood two large square buildings of transparent plastic substance. Still farther out was a sprinkling of houses, one of which the Kentons would occupy. As far as Ted could see, the ground was rust-red.

"What makes Mars so red?" Jill asked her father.

"It's believed that Mars once contained much more oxygen than it does now," the scientist replied, "and the ground was nearer the color we're used to seeing it at home. But over the centuries the oxygen was absorbed by the soil, forming iron oxide, which is the redness we see now."

"Is there any oxygen left?" Ted asked.

"Very little," replied Dr. Kenton. "That may be what caused the Martian races to disappear. This is the greatest mystery about Mars and is one of the main reasons I'm here—to discover why there are no Martians here now."

"But there're birds and animals and insects," Ted said. "Why didn't they suffocate too?"

Dr. Kenton shrugged helplessly. "Another mystery. Maybe they were able to adapt themselves to the change over the thousands of years by growing larger breathing apparatuses or something like that. Apparently, man was the one who lost out in the battle of survival."

The command to disembark came over the speaker, and the Kentons gathered up what small luggage they had kept with them and retired to the dressing room. When they had suited up with the other passengers, they entered the air lock and waited for the escalator to roll into position.

As soon as Randy's feet touched the soil moments later, Ted saw him stoop down and seize a handful of red dust and let it trickle slowly through his gloved fingers.

The commander addressed the group that was gathered around him. "It's been a pleasure to

have you people with us. This is where we part. A steward will take you over the bridge across the canal to one of the large buildings on the other side where you will register. A truck will bring your luggage over later."

As the party walked buoyantly over the ground

toward the bridge, Jill said, "I sure feel light-footed."

"You should be," her father said. "You weigh less than half of your Earth weight here. Wait until you go back to Earth after this low-gravity life. You'll be tired for about six months."

"I won't mind that," Jill answered earnestly. "I'll be so glad to get back." Ted could see that despite the excitement of their new surroundings, Jill's thoughts were still on her distant home in the Blue Ridge Mountains of Virginia.

Crossing the bridge, Ted looked over the side at the calm waters of the canal.

"This bridge is five hundred feet across and took quite a bit of engineering work," Dr. Kenton said, "but it still wasn't as big a job as the Martians did on this canal and the others all over the planet. How they built these giant waterways is another great mystery we may never know."

"Look! Aren't those the little boats you were telling us about?" Jill asked, pointing.

There were a number of tributaries extending out from the canal. It was along these that the individual houses were located.

"That's right," her father said. "We'll have a boat of our own, too."

Before leaving Earth, Dr. Kenton had explained to his family about the transportation system that connected the people with the main headquarters building of Lowell Harbor. When the colony had first been built, it was figured that the cost of fuel and cars for each individual family could be saved by making use of the natural waterways. A simple aluminum boat could run on cheaper fuel.

The new arrivals entered the nearer of the two largest buildings in the colony, and because of the compressed air inside, dared remove their helmets. In here were housed all facilities that had to do with the running of the settlement.

As they walked down the corridor to the registration room, Dr. Kenton said, "You see, the building is made entirely of panes of heavy plastic so that a hundred per cent sunlight gets in."

After registering, the Kentons were assigned their new home.

"I'm afraid you've got the house farthest out, Dr. Kenton," the clerk said. "You're the last family to arrive, and they're not building any more until more materials are sent from Earth."

"That's all right," Dr. Kenton replied. "I knew about that."

"Your boat is waiting for you outside the building at Air Lock Forty-seven," the clerk went on. "One of our men will show you how it operates and take you home. Your baggage and certain equipment for your home will be sent out later."

The Kentons walked down a long corridor to the air lock. On their way they had time to see just how many kinds of service were carried on in this most important center on Mars. If anything should happen to the functions of this building, none of the homes could survive for very long.

Outside the air lock, the Kentons found their boat awaiting them beyond a narrow strip of ground. The space-suited man inside the boat introduced himself as Martin Cooper. The Kentons climbed in and took their seats in the bottom of the boat, which was long and deep.

Ted was anxious to see how the boat was operated. He saw Mr. Cooper take a marble-sized tablet out of a box and drop it into a small tube at the rear of the boat. Then the man turned some switches. In a moment a steady popping was heard underwater, and the boat glided off.

"Is that all there is to it?" Ted asked in amazement.

"That's all," Mr. Cooper answered.

"But how does it work?" Ted wanted to know.

"The pill dissolves in the tank of water, generating a lot of pressure," Mr. Cooper replied. "It's the jet pressure that moves us along."

There was a steering wheel to guide the boat and a "gas pedal" to control the release of pressure and their speed. Mr. Cooper turned the boat into Main Canal, which was filled with other craft like their own coming and going. Presently the pilot turned out of Main Canal into a narrow waterway scarcely wider than the boat.

"This is like the 'Old Mill' run at the carnival!" Jill said, as the craft wound in and out along the irregular course.

"This boat is great fun!" Ted said. "May Jill and I run it some time, Dad?"

"I guess you'll have to when I've gone off on my expedition," Dr. Kenton answered.

"Why doesn't this water freeze?" Ted asked.

"It contains a kind of antifreeze mineral supplied by nature herself," his father said. "It never freezes, no matter how cold it gets. It's another

one of the marvels of this planet."

As they rode along, Ted was intrigued by the strange glow of the Martian sky. The thin, purplish atmosphere permitted the more brilliant stars to burn through even in the bright daylight. But then, Ted decided, it wasn't such bright daylight after all, because the faraway sun looked

91

incredibly tiny to him, and there was a sort of twilight glow to the whole scene.

Mr. Cooper guided the boat the last few feet of its journey into a little dock beside the sprawling bungalow which was to be their new home.

"End of the line!" Mr. Cooper sang out gaily. "Everyone out!"

As Mrs. Kenton was helped out by her husband, she exclaimed in a shocked tone, "Goodness! The house is made of glass! We won't have any privacy!"

"It's not glass—it's strong plastic like that in the main buildings," Dr. Kenton explained.

"And as for privacy, Mrs. Kenton, you'll have that," Mr. Cooper said. "There's a diffusing light inside the walls that makes them solid-looking when you turn on certain lights."

"I'm glad to hear that!" Mrs. Kenton said with relief.

As Mr. Cooper led them over a few feet of ground from the waterway to the house, Ted, who had been noticing the queer fixtures atop the building, asked, "What are those things up there, Mr. Cooper?"

"The network of rods and wires are the television antenna," was the reply. "That shiny disk on a pole that looks like an oversized dinner plate is your solar mirror."

Jill wanted to know what the solar mirror was.

"It collects the energy from the sun," Mr. Cooper answered patiently. "That energy in turn is what runs the generator in your home and gives you electric power."

While these explanations were going on, Randy stood fidgeting. All this was old stuff to him, and the explanations seemed to bore him.

Mr. Cooper led the party over the few feet of ground that separated the watercourse from the house. They entered a small alcove at the front of the house; this was an air lock. Mr. Cooper closed the outer door and threw a switch on the wall. Ted heard air hissing into the cramped quarters.

When this was done, the inner door was opened and the Kentons looked around the front room of their new home. The house was already oxygen-pressurized for immediate occupancy. All the furniture was of beautiful colored plastic, and waterproof, much like the styles that were popular back on Earth. The floor likewise was of poured plastic, so that the whole interior could be cleaned with a hose.

Mr. Cooper prepared to take his leave. "The things you brought from Earth and your months' food supply will be sent out in a little while. New oxygen drums are brought around once a week. If you ever need to call the headquarters building, just use the radiophone over there on the wall. Every home has its own broadcast band."

The Kentons said good-by to their guide and turned with interest to the wonders of their home. Mr. Cooper had offered to show them over the entire house, but Dr. Kenton said he had seen the plans and knew what the rest of the house was like.

There were three bedrooms in the one-floor building. Since Randy had come to live with them, Jill gave up her bedroom to the boys and agreed to take the smaller guest room.

When all had gotten acquainted with their

bedrooms, Dr. Kenton took them into the basement, which was just as large as the main floor.

"Down here are all the things that have to do with the running of our home," the scientist said. "Over there is the water tank that draws from the canal outside. The tank has a purifier in it so that the water is good to drink."

In the next room Ted found a mass of whirring dynamos and turbines. His father told them that this provided their electricity by drawing on the energy from the solar mirror. They passed down a narrow corridor. Inside one of the walls was a niche containing a large gray tank with dials on it.

"What's this?" Jill asked.

"The most precious article in the house," her father answered. "It's our oxygen drum. The air from it enters a blower that carries it evenly through the building."

The last room was the most surprising of all. Dr. Kenton opened a heavy door, and Ted, standing in front of it, gasped as a blast of frigid air hit him. He saw his father grinning. "That gives you an idea of how cold the ground is," Dr. Kenton said. "This is a natural deepfreeze. It never varies more than a few degrees all year 'round."

His shivering companions took a moment to look inside. Ted saw a room as large as the upstairs living room. It was empty.

"When they bring our food, this place will be a third full," Dr. Kenton said.

"Do you mean to say I have to come downstairs and go into that cold place every time I want a stick of butter?" Mrs. Kenton asked unhappily.

Dr. Kenton merely grinned at her. He led them back upstairs and into the kitchen. He opened one of several doors built right into the wall. Frigid air seeped out of the compartment just as it had downstairs.

"This is our regular refrigerator," Dr. Kenton said. "It connects by pipe to the basement freezer."

"I'm glad to know that," Mrs. Kenton returned, with a smile of relief. "I thought I'd have to trot myself to death going up and down those basement steps."

Ted thought what fun it was going to be living in their very own home on this distant planet. Wouldn't he have exciting things to tell the kids back on Earth when he returned?

CHAPTER NINE

A Cry in the Night

HOURS LATER, Ted lay awake in the upper bunk of the double-deck bed he shared with Randy. The foam-rubber mattress under him was soft as a cloud, and the cool artificial air of the house inflated his lungs satisfyingly.

But though he was comfortable, Ted could not sleep. He had lain awake for an hour. He guessed it was because of the excitement of the past few days and the fact that this was his first night on solid ground after months of life in space.

He climbed down the ladder to the floor, quietly so as not to disturb Randy. He stared through the clear plastic walls of his room at the hushed Martian night. The sky was a glittering canopy of starlight. Phobos, the fleet closer moon, cast a weak light over the landscape. Beyond their desert back yard, Ted saw the dark spreading mass of the sand bog which he had been warned about. It was like quicksand and would draw anything that touched it down to destruction. Ringing the bog Ted saw thick clusters of white flowers, which his father had said was a favorite food of the little Martian color bears.

Ted had also learned that the animals fed at night. He wondered if any of the creatures were in these parts, and if there were any chance he would see one of them. He kept his eyes on the bog for what seemed an hour, but he caught no sign of movement down there. At last his eyes grew blurry and he thought he could sleep. He turned away and climbed the ladder.

Just as his lids closed, something startled him, and he jerked up in bed. He wasn't sure what had aroused him. He sat there in the semidarkness, his heart bumping rapidly, his ears alerted.

Then he heard a sound. It seemed far off. It

was like a wail, a cry. He came down the ladder again. In his haste, he tripped on the bottom rung and went sprawling. He turned anxiously toward the bed and saw Randy sit up.

"I'm sorry, Randy," Ted said. "I thought I heard something outdoors."

"I heard it, too," Randy said.

The two looked outside, straining their eyes to pierce the shadowy night. Suddenly Randy whispered tensely, "There!"

Ted stared where he pointed. There was a figure at the edge of the bog. They heard the sound repeated. It seemed to be coming from the moving figure. Ted suddenly remembered his father's field glasses lying on a table in his parents' room. Before going to bed, all of them had used them to study the stars.

Ted tiptoed down the hall into his parents' room. Carefully he lifted the glasses from the table and returned to his own room. He could hardly wait to train the glasses on the mysterious thing beside the bog.

"Did you hear it again?" Ted asked as he swept his glasses over the landscape.

Randy nodded. "It sounded like a color bear. He must be in trouble."

Finally Ted found what he was looking for. He was able to make out a little furry body struggling at the bog's edge. The animal appeared to be trapped in the marsh. One stubby paw was grasping a root growing out of the bank. Ted handed the glasses to Randy.

"It's a color bear," Randy whispered. "He's stuck in the bog. He'll never get out by himself."

Ted saw a wistful look on Randy's face. "I sure

hate to see anything happen to those little fellows. They're so friendly."

"You mean they make good pets?" Ted wanted to know.

"They sure do," Randy answered. "I owned one once, until he fell into a bog. It seems they always end up in one sooner or later."

"I wonder if we could help him," Ted suggested.

"It may be dangerous," Randy warned. "If we should slip. . . ."

"You've been around them before, haven't you?"

"Yes."

"I'm willing to try it if you are," Ted said.

"Let's go then."

"We'll have to be careful not to wake the others," Ted said.

Softly they crept down the hall to the spacesuit closet. Silently they dressed and inflated their suits with oxygen. Then they went through the air lock and on outdoors.

Ted had brought a flashlight. The cone of

whiteness fanned out ahead of them, leading the way for them over the red sands. As they drew near the sand bog, the wails of the trapped animal became louder and more frantic.

"We'd better hurry," Randy said. "He may go down any moment."

They broke into a run and finally reached the side of the little fellow. The only part of him visible now was his round head, from which projected big cup-handle ears. His short forepaws still clung to the root, but even now the boys could see his grip loosening.

As they knelt beside him, they saw his violet button eyes turned pleadingly up to them.

"The bank seems firm," Randy said. "Let's brace ourselves and each take one of his paws."

The black mud pulled strongly against them. After a few moments the boys' arms ached from the tug of war, but they appeared to be winning the battle. Slowly the bear rose out of his trap. Just as Ted thought his own arms would be pulled off from the strain, the animal sucked free of the clutching slime and came tumbling up over Ted and Randy.

As the boys climbed to their feet, the color bear ran up first to one and then to the other, and licked their helmets gratefully with his long red tongue!

The little creature stood about two and a half

feet tall and was so roly-poly, he must have been nearly that wide. The mud caked his body, some of it crawling like thick molasses down into a black puddle around his flat feet. He walked upright just as they did.

"What'll we do with him?" Randy asked.

"Let him go, I guess," Ted replied. "I wish we could keep him, but I'm afraid Dad wouldn't agree. For some reason, he doesn't like color bears. Besides, there's no place to keep him."

They walked back toward the house. Presently Ted turned and saw what he had feared. The bear was trudging along behind. They tried to shoo him off. This only made him hesitate momentarily and then start following again. Finally they gave up, permitting him to trail along at a distance.

When they reached the air lock, they opened the door. As they waited for the pressure to come up, the color bear stood outside looking in at them. Ted thought he had the most plaintive expression he had ever seen. It was almost human.

"We can't let him stand out there like that all night," Ted said. "He might wake up the whole house with his cries. They do cry, don't they?"

"Just like babies," Randy said.

"I forgot, though," Ted said. "They can't breathe our air mixture, can they?"

"Yes, they can." Randy told him. "They have

a valve in their bodies that takes care of that."

"I believe we can wash that goo off him and leave him in the kitchen until morning," Ted said. "Maybe he'll be quiet if he's clean."

They let the bear in, and in appreciation he licked their helmets again.

"If you want to stay in here, you'll have to be quiet," Randy warned, just as though the animal could understand.

"Hey!" Ted cried. "What's wrong with him?" The little animal was reeling around as though he could hardly keep his feet, and his eyes were glazed.

"They always do that the first few times they enter our atmosphere," Randy answered.

The color bear adjusted himself quickly to the change and then seemed all right again. Quietly the boys led him down the hall toward the shower. In the bathroom they shut the door, removed their helmets and turned on the shower in a gentle spray. The bear did not take to water willingly, and the boys had to force him under. When he began squealing and kicking, Ted put his hand over his mouth. As the little animal felt the warm water, however, his broad mouth turned upward in a grin, and he sat down in the middle of the plastic basin to enjoy his bath.

While the mud was washing down the drain Ted began to see what a beautiful creature the color bear really was. His soft fur was white next to the body, then merged into reddish brown at the tip. To make him even more colorful, his paws, legs, and head had a bluish tinge. "What a patriotic creature he would be on Earth," Ted thought. He had all the colors of the American flag.

When the animal was clean, Ted got out a blotting towel that dried the bear in a matter of seconds. The little fellow looked happy after his bath and grinned at them. When he tried to lick their bare faces, they had to cover up. He seemed hurt by their gesture and pouted for a moment, with his lower lip quivering.

"See what I mean?" Randy said, grinning. "They're almost human."

"I wish we could keep him," Ted said longingly. "He seems like lots of fun. I think I'll ask Dad about it."

As they were cleaning up the bathroom, Ted, who was leaning over the shower basin, felt Randy's hand press sharply on his shoulder. Ted spun around. Standing in the doorway was his father, a stern look on his face.

CHAPTER TEN

School on Mars

W HAT IN THE WORLD are you two doing?"
Dr. Kenton asked.

Ted told him the whole story of the rescue,
ending up with a request that they keep the
Martian animal for a pet.

Ted's father shook his head. "That's impossible. There's no place to keep him." His face grew
stern again. "You two did a very foolish thing
going out alone near that bog. You might have
fallen in. I want you to promise that you won't
go near that place again."

They promised. Ted knew it was no use arguing about keeping the color bear. When his father made up his mind, he rarely changed it.

111

As the three walked along the hallway with the bear, Dr. Kenton said, "You kids woke me up with all that splashing in the bathroom, but, fortunately, Mom is still asleep. We must be quiet so that we won't waken her and Jill."

The bear was reluctant to be forced out of the house through the air lock. Ted knew the animal felt no worse than he did. He had become quite attached to the little fellow in even this short time.

When the bear was outside in the dark, he looked mournfully through the transparent doors at his former friends who had rejected him. Then he began wailing softly. Ted looked hopefully at his father, wishing that he would have a change of heart. But Dr. Kenton's expression was set, and Ted knew there was no chance of the color bear coming back inside.

The three of them retired to bed, but Ted was a long time getting to sleep. For almost an hour the Martian creature kept up a soft wail. Ted covered up his ears with his air-filled pillow, and he was finally able to drop off to sleep.

The next morning Ted and Randy went to the front door the first thing after they rose. There was no sign of the color bear.

"I guess he finally gave up," said Ted unhappily.

"I can't understand his being alone like he was," Randy said. "Usually the little bears travel around in families of about ten. I guess this one was an orphan."

Hearing this, Ted felt even worse. "Maybe a wild animal got him," he murmured. "If it hasn't already, it probably will sooner or later. By the way, what kind of wild animals do they have here?"

"None of them ever come close to the colony," Randy answered. "Hundreds of miles away, there's the Great Martian Forest where all kinds of them live. One of the fiercest kinds are the elephant ants. Big herds of blue rovers run across the desert closer by. There are different kinds of birds here, too."

"I've heard of a dangerous plant in the Great Forest," Ted said. "What's it called?"

"The whip tree," Randy answered. "It throws tentacles around anything that's near and draws it into its center mouth."

Realizing the dangers to the lonely little bear, Ted had not much appetite for breakfast. Neither of the boys nor Dr. Kenton had mentioned the adventure of the night before, but Mrs. Kenton had heard some noises, although they had thought she was asleep. She began asking questions and finally got the whole story.

"I wish we could have kept that little animal!" Jill sighed. "He sounds wonderful!"

"We can't adopt every stray animal that comes along," Dr. Kenton said. "I'm sure the color bear will get back to his family all right. He probably just strayed temporarily."

Dr. Kenton next said that he was going to report to the science organization this morning. He asked the children if they wanted to go along and register in school. They'd have to within the next few days anyhow.

"Are the schools like they are back home?" Jill asked.

"They sure are," her father said. "Just as modern as you'll find anywhere."

Hearing this, the children were eager to go. Schools in the twenty-first century were a combination of wholesome entertainment and instruction. No dry textbooks or cramped wooden desks with hard seats. Ted and Jill had heard about the poor children of the mid-1900's who had to plod through school with such handicaps as these, and they felt sorry for them.

Ted noticed that Dad seemed reluctant to leave Mom by herself, but she did not seem to mind.

"Don't worry about me," Mrs. Kenton said merrily. "I'll have plenty to do unpacking our clothes and things that they dumped in the living room yesterday. I won't even miss you *four*

and Dr. Kenton went
o   s, Ted saw that the sun
w   the horizon. He had
le   early on Mars to take
a   th and illumination of

115

Dr. Kenton looked into the purple sky through which the stars gleamed. "It's exactly six-fifteen now," he said.

"How did you know that?" Ted asked in surprise. "You didn't look at your watch."

"I didn't have to," his father answered. "That little disk in the sky gives it to me."

"That's Phobos," Ted supplied.

"Right," his father answered. "It takes only six hours for the moon to go from one horizon to the other, so you can actually see its movement in a few minutes' time. By judging its distance from the star around it, I can get the time."

"That sure must take a lot of knowledge of the stars to know just where each one should be at any one time!" Ted said.

"It does," the scientist replied, "but you'll learn it in school. I'll bet Randy knows how to do it now. How about it, Randy?"

"Yes sir," Randy replied with a grin, "but I guess I'm a little off after being away so long. I thought the time was six-thirty."

Dr. Kenton took another look, and Ted could see his face redden inside his helmet. "I'm the

one who's a little bit off, Randy!" he admitted.
"It *is* six-thirty."

Suddenly Jill cried, "Ooo—look!"

A half dozen large birds were swooping down
on the boat. Dr. Kenton did not appear alarmed
—only amused. "They won't hurt us," he said.
"They're whee birds and very friendly."

The beautiful birds folded their scarlet wings,
tipped in yellow, and perched on the sides of the
boat. Then they began giving out a peculiar,
"Whee-whee," as though they were enjoying the
boat ride.

"Don't they sound funny!" Ted said.

The birds soared away as the boat turned into
Main Canal. A few minutes later, Dr. Kenton
drove up to the building they had registered in
the day before. But instead of docking at the
building, Dr. Kenton continued along the canal
beside the building in the direction of the other
large building next to it.

"We're going to the science building today,"
the scientist explained.

"Why is that as big as the administration
building?" Jill asked.

The birds soared away.

"Don't forget, Jill, that science and research is our main business on Mars," Dr. Kenton told her. "Every imaginable research project is carried on there. Your schoolroom is there, too."

Dr. Kenton docked the boat at the science building, and the four got out and entered. When they had removed their space suits, Dr. Kenton took the children to the school superintendent's office, where he left them. The superintendent had them fill out cards, and then he took them down a hall.

"We have only a hundred and fifty students enrolled, so we don't need many classrooms," he said, and stopped before one of the rooms, knocking on the door.

A dark-haired young man opened it, and the superintendent introduced him to the children as their teacher, Mr. Garland. He assigned the newcomers seats, and since school had already begun for the day, he went on with his lesson.

The room darkened, and a regular three-dimensional color movie flashed on the screen. It was a picture about the wonders of the Earth. Ted felt a lump rise in his throat as he watched.

119

What he was looking at was the Natural Bridge in Virginia, not far from their old home. Ted looked at Jill. A stray pencil of light from the camera showed tears glistening in her eyes. Ted was feeling a wave of homesickness himself. The wonders of Mars were exciting, but there was no substitute in all the universe for their own little plot of ground on Earth where they had been born.

Ted was glad when the movie was over and another subject was taken up. With slides, Mr. Garland demonstrated the geography of Mars. Ted learned that the red planet was mostly a vast stretch of desert through which ran the marvelous network of canals. Mr. Garland likened the climate of Mars to that atop a high mountain on earth—the air thin and cold.

Ted was glad when the recreation period came and he could exercise.

It was his first such opportunity since leaving Earth. In the boys' gym the athletic instructor was teaching the game of basketball. Some of the students like Randy had been born on Mars and knew nothing at all about the game. Ted said that he had played a lot of it in school back on Earth and volunteered to help the instructor, who was glad of the assistance.

When school was out, the young Kentons and Randy reported to the science-building office, where Dr. Kenton was waiting for them.

"Did you get your assignment?" Jill asked.

"Yes," he replied. "I'll be leaving you in a few days. We're going on an expedition to Hellespontus, where some mysterious fossils have been discovered. They may be bones of the ancient Martians. If so, they could solve the baffling riddle of what happened to those remarkable canal builders."

After getting into space clothes, they went to their boat and started homeward. As they approached their isolated house at the end of the winding watercourse, Ted rose in his seat and pointed.

"Look!" he exclaimed. "There's the color bear again!"

Sure enough, seated on the front doorstep, as though waiting for them to return, was the little Martian animal they had rescued the night before.

CHAPTER ELEVEN

Yank

"I SN'T HE THE CUTEST THING!" exclaimed Jill, as she saw the red-white-and-blue creature.

"I thought we were rid of him," Dr. Kenton groaned.

He brought the boat to the end of the waterway and tied it up. The children leaped out and ran to the bear, who climbed to his chubby feet to greet them. He licked the suits of Ted and Randy but merely stared at Jill and Dr. Kenton.

"It looks like we just can't get rid of him," Ted said, renewing his hope for possession of the animal.

"Oh, Father, can't we keep him?" Jill pleaded, stroking the color bear.

Randy patted the little round head, and the bear made a sort of purring, contented sound as the children fondled him.

Dr. Kenton threw up his hands helplessly. "I guess I know when I'm licked!" he burst out. "If Mother agrees, we'll try and keep him. But you kids will have to attend to him yourselves, and mind you keep him out of the sand bog, or you won't have him long."

"We will!" Jill said. Now that she had made friends with the bear, he seemed ready to accept her and licked her suit as a sign of friendship.

Randy stayed outside with the bear while the other children went inside to talk persuasively with their mother. She objected at first, but finally yielded to their persistence.

"We'll have to make out a requisition for plastic material for his outdoor house," Dr. Kenton said. "Are you children willing to chip in part of your allowance to pay for it?"

They nodded.

"We'll order it the same time as we do supplies for the garden," the scientist said.

"We're going to have a garden?" Jill burst out.

"I thought we'd try it," her father said. "That's the only way we can get fresh vegetables."

When Dr. Kenton went to the study to make out the requisition slip, Ted asked his mother, "Why didn't Dad want to keep the bear? It seems to me that he doesn't like those little guys, or is afraid of them, or something."

"As a matter of fact, he is a little shy of them, I believe," she answered. "He accidentally hurt a baby one badly in one of his explorations a few years ago, when he crushed its forepaw under his boot and it ran off crying. Your father's so tenderhearted he's probably reminded of that painful incident every time he sees one of the animals."

"Maybe he'll change after the bear has been around for a while," Jill put in.

The air-lock door opened, and Randy stuck his head in.

"We'd forgotten all about you, Randy!" Jill exclaimed.

"Are we going to keep him?" Randy asked anxiously.

"We sure are!" Jill piped. "Bring him in and let's introduce him to Mother."

Randy let the color bear inside. When he began staggering about, Mrs. Kenton exclaimed with horror: "He's dying, the poor little fellow."

Randy assured her he wasn't really—that he behaved like this because of the extra oxygen in the air. Randy said that before long the bear would be able to go in and out without any bad effects at all.

Ted brought the animal over to his mother. She gingerly patted his blue furry head. In response he licked her dress. "Now we're friends," Mrs. Kenton said.

"We've got to give him a name," Jill said. "What'll we call him?"

"How about Fuzzy?" suggested Mrs. Fenton.

"No. Teddy!" Jill said.

Ted wrinkled his nose. "Then you'd get him mixed up with me. I think he ought to have a patriotic name because of his colors."

"How about Yank, then?" Mrs. Kenton said.

"That's a good one!" Jill agreed.

"Yeah, that's swell!" Ted said. "What do you think, Randy?"

He shrugged and grinned. "It sounds all right to me, but I don't know what it means."

Ted explained the word as being sort of a nickname for America and Americans. Randy had learned quite a bit about the United States flag, but the word Yankee was a new one to him. After he learned its meaning, he agreed that Yank was a perfect name for the color bear. When Dr. Kenton returned, Ted felt that the final introduction to the newest member of their family should be made.

"Yank, meet Dr. Kenton," Ted said formally.

Ted's father smiled and approached the little animal. "Hi, Yank," he said.

His hand went out to pat the round head, but to everyone's surprise, Yank drew back with a cry of fright. Dr. Kenton's face went red as if he had been snubbed by a human being. Ted felt sorry for his father. Did the bear unconsciously know what the scientist had done to another member of his kind?

"Don't worry, John," Mrs. Kenton said soothingly. "He'll come around to you before long."

Her husband quickly changed the subject. "I've made out the requisitions. I'll send them over to headquarters now on the video-sender."

The children watched interestedly as he went to the video-sender, which was connected to the radiophone. He fastened the slips face down on a glass plate and held open a switch for several seconds. About a minute later, a buzz came over the radiophone.

"That means it's been received," Dr. Kenton said. "I asked to have it sent to us tomorrow."

"Why couldn't you just phone it in?" Ted asked.

"This way there doesn't have to be anyone on the other end," his father explained. "The requisition was handled by an automatic machine."

Yank was given temporary quarters in the basement. Dr. Kenton said he could not live indefinitely inside like this—that an outside shelter was absolutely necessary.

The next afternoon after school, Dr. Kenton brought the children home. Sitting outside the house on the ground were two pieces of specially formed plastic.

"Here are the things we ordered," Dr. Kenton said. "The manufacturers shaped them on molds they already have on hand."

The color bear's house was a rounded dome resembling an Eskimo igloo. The garden shelter was oval and about twenty-five feet long.

"How are we going to lift those things?" Ted asked. "They must be awfully heavy!"

"On the contrary, they're quite light," Dr.

Kenton said. "Each of you grab a handle on the side of the garden top and I'll show you."

They discovered they could lift the large object with ease. They carried it around the house, and Dr. Kenton showed how it would fit close to the wall. The entrance would be by way of the back door.

"The dome is double-walled!" Ted said.

"Of course, it is," Dr. Kenton answered. "So is our house—and all the buildings on Mars."

"Why?" Ted asked.

"For insulation against the cold," was the reply. "The outer wall gets almost as cold as the temperature outside, but the vacuum between it and the inner wall keeps the inside nice and warm."

"The walls are so clear in the house, I never noticed they were double," Ted said.

"Shall we get started on the garden?" Dr. Kenton asked. "The sooner we get it in shape, the sooner we can grow tomatoes and beans and dwarf fruit trees."

They first went into the house, where Mrs.

Kenton showed them a large pile of supplies that had been sent along with the shelter tops.

"Here's a foam-rubber mattress for Yank," the scientist said, pulling out two bundles, "and a supply of food for him. Everything else is for the garden."

The first thing the four of them did outside was set up Yank's house, close to the front door, and lay out his sleeping mat. When this was done, the little animal walked cautiously inside and sniffed all around. Then he curled up on the soft cushion and closed his eyes.

"He seems satisfied with it," said Jill.

First work on the garden was to air-seal it to the rear of the house. This was done with a strange-looking gun that shot a thick gluey liquid out along the seams between the plastic cover and the house. The rest of the work had to be done under the dome itself. The workers went back indoors and hauled all the equipment under the garden shelter.

"First we bring the warm house atmosphere into here, so that we can remove our space gear," Dr. Kenton said.

When this was done, and with their space suits off, the workers could move about more efficiently.

"After supper we'll prepare the ground, and tomorrow we can plant seeds," Dr. Kenton said.

Ted thumped the hard, cold ground with his shoe. "How can we work this?" he asked. "It's hard as stone, and it must be awfully cold."

His father pulled some long steel spikes out of the mass of equipment. Then he took out a sledge hammer. He hammered the spikes at intervals in the ground along the sides of the dome. Then he attached an electrical circuit to each of them and the whole to a generator.

As the generator purred in operation, he said, "Infrared heat rays are being sent out by the spikes into the ground, warming it. After supper the ground will be thawed out so that we can till it."

When they returned to the garden area after their last meal of the day, they found that the ground could be worked easily. Electric tools made the job quick and efficient. Fertilizer and soil conditioner were worked into the ground after the surface had been loosened up for several feet down.

"Did you say we could plant seeds tomorrow?" Jill asked, when they were through.

"That's right," her father replied. "The chemicals we have put in the ground are almost miraculous in the speed with which they work in the soil. They can literally do the job overnight."

Jill and Ted went to bed tired and untroubled that night. But not Randy. Before Ted dropped off, he heard Randy tossing restlessly in the bunk below. Ted caught some of the words muttered by the boy: "Father . . . miss you . . . ever come back to me?"

They had been kept so busy during those first days in their new home that Ted had almost forgotten that Randy wasn't his brother. Randy seemed to have taken to the family very well, Ted thought, but he realized no foster parents could take the place of his real father. As Ted fell asleep, he was thinking what an unhappy day it was going to be for all of them when Randy found out that his father was never going to return.

CHAPTER TWELVE

Illness Strikes

THE YOUNG FOLKS planted seeds the next afternoon when they came home from school. Then in the next few days, they could scarcely wait to see the first seedlings break through the soil. The little green crooks popped up the morning that Dr. Kenton was to leave on his expedition.

The scientist said that the plants would grow rapidly and produce edible food within the next ten days. He gave the children instructions for tending the crops, and they memorized his directions.

He had showed Jill, Ted, and Randy how to attend to the mechanical functions of the home and also how to run the boat. The three helped him to load his gear into the boat, and then stood by as Dr. Kenton bade farewell to his wife. There were tears in Mrs. Kenton's eyes as she waved good-by from inside the house.

Yank watched the strange goings-on from in front of his own dwelling. He seemed to understand that Dr. Kenton was leaving, but he still had not made friends with him.

When they were all in the boat, Jill dropped a fuel pill into the tank, and Ted took the steering wheel. He skillfully guided the boat along the winding watercourse to Main Canal and along its length to the science building. They all helped unload the gear on the dock, and Dr. Kenton said that this was where they must part.

"You three will have to run things while I'm away," the scientist told them. "You shouldn't have any trouble, but if anything does happen, call headquarters for help. There's one thing I want you to be sure to attend to. Bring the empty spare air cartridges in the closet down here and have them filled. You never know when you'll need them."

"We'll bring them tomorrow on our way to school," Ted promised.

Jill hugged her father hard and long. Like her mother, she was tearful at his leaving. Ted, himself, felt a tug of dread. He wondered if the trip into the Martian wilds would be a successful one or whether, as in the case of Randy's father, it would end in disaster.

The children went on to school. Ted was glad to be going because it would take his and Jill's minds off the melancholy of their father's departure.

Ted found the opening lesson particularly interesting. In it he learned facts about the extinct native Martians. Mr. Garland showed slides on some diggings that had unearthed bones of these early people. The bones had been organized to the best of Earth scientists' ability, but many were missing, and the reconstructed figures were largely guesswork. Ted wondered if his father's expedition would uncover more information on these mysterious ancient people.

As the young Kentons and Randy started for home in the boat that afternoon, Jill complained of having a headache. Ted told her it was probably due to eyestrain from looking at the slides, and this seemed to satisfy her. But when Ted docked the boat at the house, Jill said she felt worse.

Yank came running out to greet them, but the boys were so concerned over Jill that they paid little attention to him. He stood off sulking and watched Ted help his sister out of the boat and through the air lock of their house.

"Mother, Jill is sick!" Ted called when they were inside.

Mrs. Kenton had been spraying the hose on the plastic floor and furniture. She turned it off and allowed the spring on the hose to pull it back into the wall opening. The water swirled through the drain in the center of the floor and disappeared in a matter of seconds.

"What's wrong with her?" Mrs. Kenton asked in alarm.

Ted helped Jill off with her helmet. He was shocked to see that her face was feverish and her eyes strangely bright. She wandered away from the others and slumped tiredly on the divan.

"Don't lie on that rubber cushion, dear!" Mrs. Kenton cried. "It's still wet. What on earth has she got?" Mrs. Kenton asked the boys.

"It looks to me like she's got bog fever," Randy offered.

"How could she catch fever?" Mrs. Kenton asked.

"There's a virus that comes from the sand bogs and sometimes gets through the air valve of space suits," Randy said.

"I'd better call a doctor at headquarters right away!" Mrs. Kenton declared.

She went to the radiophone and put through the call. She was told that all the doctors were out on calls and that it might be an hour before one could come. However, when a nurse on duty in the Medical Center learned about Jill's symptoms, she gave instructions for caring for the girl until the doctor could come.

As Mrs. Kenton switched off the phone, she said, "The nurse said that Jill should be put to bed and kept warm. Come on, Honey," she added, helping Jill to her feet and leading her toward the guest room.

"Is the disease serious?" Ted asked Randy worriedly.

"It can be," Randy answered soberly. "We'll probably have to be quarantined," he added.

"How long does bog fever last?" Ted asked.

"The crisis comes pretty quickly after the first attack," Randy answered. "I remember, because a friend of mine had it. If they pass the crisis, they're usually well in a few days."

Ted was reluctant to ask the next question, but he felt he must know.

"Did your friend recover, Randy?"

Randy shook his head, and Ted felt a cold chill of dread run down his spine. He didn't know what he'd do if something happened to Jill. She *had* to get well.

About twenty minutes later, Mrs. Kenton came back to the living room. Her face was drawn and worried.

"She's sleeping fitfully and her head is burning up!" she told the boys. "Oh, why doesn't that doctor come?"

With nothing else to do, the boys stared through the clear plastic of the side wall at the deepening afternoon. The purple sky was growing darker, and the stars were gleaming steadily brighter. On the horizon, where the miniature sun was setting, the sky was painted in gorgeous shades of red. Ted thought he had never seen a more beautiful sunset, but he could not appreciate it at this time.

Suddenly Ted spotted a strange yellow mass gliding close to the ground and apparently coming in the direction of the settlement.

"What's that, Randy?" Ted asked. "Do you know?"

"We're in for trouble!" Randy answered.

"What do you mean?" Ted asked, alarmed.

"It's a dust storm blowing this way," Randy said.

"I'm glad the house is well anchored to the ground," Ted muttered. He had already learned in school that such storms were often fierce.

"It may be an awful blow," Randy said. "It may keep the doctor from getting through to us."

Once more Ted had that sinking feeling. He

The whole landscape was blotted out.

wished desperately that there were something he could do. But, against the powers of nature, he knew he was absolutely helpless. All he and Randy could do was wait and hope.

A few minutes later the dust storm struck with howling fury. The boys watched the sand spatter noisily against the house. The whole landscape was blotted out in a blinding, yellowish-red haze. Mrs. Kenton came running into the room, looking terrified. She had not been prepared for this latest trouble.

"How long will this terrible storm last?" she asked, when Randy explained what it was.

"Sometimes as long as an hour," Randy replied.

Mrs. Kenton's hands twisted in frenzy. "We can't wait that long. We must have that doctor. Poor Jill is twisting and turning so much, I can't even keep damp cloths on her forehead."

"Why don't we call headquarters again," Ted suggested, "and see if the doctor will be able to come out in the storm."

As Mrs. Kenton went into the hall to radiophone again, the boys heard the storm striking with renewed power. Fine, cutting sand whipped against the plastic walls with the sound of sleet, accompanied by an eerie roar.

Mrs. Kenton came back quickly. "There's no sound at all over the phone!" she cried.

Ted instantly thought of the aerial on top of the house. He went to the center room and looked through the clear ceiling. His heart sank. The aerial was swinging loose by the single center pole.

"The storm has blown the antenna loose!" Ted told his mother. "We can't even phone headquarters now, and they can't reach us either."

Mrs. Kenton left the room, moaning. They heard her go down the hall to Jill's room. The only sound was the furious clatter of sand against the house and the groaning of the terrible wind. Ted's eyes strained to detect some kind of break in that awful cloud of yellow dust that surrounded the house, hoping that the storm was nearing its end.

Suddenly Ted heard a weak sound outside, above the roar of the wind. "Yank!" he cried.

"We forgot all about Yank! We've got to let him in!"

They ran to the front-door air lock. There they found the color bear clawing at the outer door. The dust covered him so thickly that he nearly blended completely with the yellowish background.

Ted flipped a switch opening the outer door. Yank scrambled quickly inside. Then, when the air pressure in the little outer compartment was equal to that in the house, Ted opened the inner door. Yank tumbled in in a flurry of scattering sand.

Ted thought the Martian animal was the most forlorn sight he had ever seen. His fur was dirty and matted, his eyes were bloodshot, and every step he took brought a cascade of sand down around his feet.

"He looks like he needs another shower," Randy said.

"There's nothing else we can do now," Ted agreed. Besides, he figured the activity would take his mind off their troubles.

Mrs. Kenton was still with Jill. The boys

marched Yank down the hallway to the bath-room. When Yank saw what was in store for him, he eagerly jumped into the shower basin. Ted turned on the water, and streams of dark-red liquid poured down Yank into the drain.

"He must have half the sand of Mars on him," Ted commented.

Suddenly his mother came up to the door and looked in. "Jill's getting worse!" she said. "Ted, you and Randy must go out after the doctor."

CHAPTER THIRTEEN

News for Randy

TED WAS NOT KEEN to venture out into the dust storm, but thoughts of his sister lying desperately ill quickly drove all hesitation from his mind. He and Randy climbed into their space suits, and as they approached the front-door air lock, Ted was relieved to find that he could begin to see through the thinning dust.

"It'll be over in a few minutes now," Randy said.

But if Ted expected any easy time of it outdoors, he was mistaken. The storm still had a lot of fight left in it. The wind struck them relentlessly, turning them around and blinding their gaze with whirling dust. They could not even thrust through it to the boat. Ted signaled to Randy that they would have to stand close to the house until the storm had subsided even more.

At last the wind died to gusts. The air was clearer now, and the stars were once again visible overhead.

"I think we can make it now," Ted said.

They ran over to the boat and climbed in. As Ted dropped a pellet into the tank, Randy said, "Look at these scratches on the boat! That sand must cut like a file!"

They jetted off down the waterway, Ted pressing the accelerator pedal down to shove the boat along as fast as it could safely go. They whirled into the Main Canal and sped toward the science building where the doctors had their offices. Along the way, the boys could see that theirs wasn't the only aerial that had been blown down. They could see space-suited figures on the individual houses working on the webs of wires and poles.

Some whee birds appeared out of nowhere and flew down to perch on the boat and serenade Ted and Randy with their strange chants. However, the boys were in no mood for them now, and presently the friendly birds flapped off as though they realized they were not wanted.

Before reaching the building, the boys saw a boat speeding right at them.

"Look out!" Randy warned. "He's coming straight at us."

But the boat pulled up just beside the craft occupied by Ted and Randy.

"Are you the Kenton family?" the single occupant asked over his radio.

"Yes, sir!" Ted answered quickly. "Are you the doctor?"

"Yes," the man answered. "The storm has held me up. How's your sister, Son?"

"She's bad off, sir," Ted answered. "That's why I had to come for you."

"Turn your boat around and don't spare the horses, as they used to say," the doctor said. "I'll be right behind you."

Ted made the fastest trip yet along the waterway back home. True to his word, the doctor arrived right at his heels. The doctor jumped out of his boat at the house, grabbed up a large case, and hurried toward the air lock. The boys went ahead and opened the door for him.

When the doctor had met Mrs. Kenton inside, he asked to see the sick girl alone. The boys and Mrs. Kenton paced restlessly in the front room as they waited for the doctor to come out of Jill's room. Finally, when Ted thought he could not stand the waiting any longer, the doctor came out. He was briskly shaking down a thermometer, and his face was bland.

"She'll be a sick girl for a few days," he said, "but she'll be all right. I gave her a shot of some special serum we developed to combat bog fever. It was none too soon, either."

There were tears of joy on Mrs. Kenton's face, and Ted felt as though he could turn handsprings. Randy, too, looked vastly relieved. Although he was not a true member of the family, it seemed as though Ted and Jill were brother and sister to him, especially since he had no brother or sister of his own.

"I'm afraid all of you will have to be quarantined for a week," the doctor went on.

"What'll we ever find to do with ourselves staying in the house for a whole week?" Ted thought. Then he remembered the garden that had to be tended, that antenna that had to be repaired, and other mechanical duties that had to do with the running of the house. If they kept busy, the time would pass swiftly, he reasoned. The boys went up on the roof to try to repair the antenna, but there was such a tangle of wires they did not know where to start. The doctor said he would leave word at headquarters for a repairman to come out.

"It may be a day or so before he can get out here, though," the doctor warned. "It looks as though half the aerials in the settlement were blown down."

It was actually two days before a repairman came. By that time, Jill had passed her worst time, and she was able to sit up a little and see the boys.

Ted and Randy were amazed at the rapid growth of the plants in the garden. Already they were eighteen inches high. Ted thought he could almost see them growing before his eyes.

As soon as the radiomen had repaired the antenna, the boys sat down to watch the television program in progress. It was a newscast that showed in color the events going on all the way back on Earth and within the settlement as well. The huge five-by-four-foot screen was sharp and clear.

Suddenly the regular telecast was interrupted. A local announcer was switched in. He held a paper in his hand, and by the expression on his face, Ted knew he had something very important to say.

"Ladies and gentlemen," the announcer said, "we have just received word that several members of the long-lost expedition to Syrtis Major have been spotted and contacted by a routine surveying plane. That is all the information we can give you now, but stand by and we'll keep you posted on developments."

Randy had sprung to his feet, and Ted could see his body was tense as a coil of wire.

"Pops!" Randy burst out.

"Your father's expedition!" Ted exclaimed at the same moment. Then before his hopes got too high, he recalled that the announcer had said that only some of the men had been found.

But Randy did not appear to be bothered by this. His face glowed with happiness. He was convinced his father was one of those who had been located.

An hour later, another bulletin was given: "It has been established that only six of the original thirty-five members of the ill-fated expedition are alive. Identity of the men has not yet been given us. Stand by for further news."

Randy bit his lip in disappointment as the message was cut off. He and Ted remained by the set for another hour without moving, hoping any moment that more news would be given out. At last it came:

"Our remote TV facilities will carry you to the spot where the lost men were found," the announcer said. There was a gray screen for several moments, and then the scene switched to the interior of a rocket plane.

"It'll be just like our going along with them to the place!" Randy exclaimed happily.

Ted kept his fingers crossed for Randy. It

would be a terrible shock to him if his father were not one of the survivors. The unhappy moment he had dreaded for so long might now be at hand. Their screen showed the swift trip from Lowell Harbor over red sands and lichen forests. At last the plane came in for landing in a wild, rocky region.

The man who met the TV men in the plane was the pilot who had first sighted the missing engineers. "Come with me," the pilot said, "and I'll show you who the survivors are and we'll hear their story."

Ted saw Randy get up and move close to the screen. He saw Randy's toe beat a nervous tattoo against the floor as he waited. Mrs. Kenton had come into the room in the meantime, when she found what was going on. Even Jill could hardly be restrained from leaving her bed to come in and take part in the great discovery that meant so much to young Randy Matthews.

"The men survived by holing up in an underground cave, and they signaled the scouting plane," the pilot explained, as he led the TV men over the rocky ground. "It was a landslide

154

that broke up the expedition, destroying all means of transportation and communication. The six who lived through it gathered up all the spare oxygen tanks and food supplies. They had plenty along because the expedition was to have lasted three months. They carried the tanks underground where a hot spring kept them warm."

When the entrance to the cave was reached, the pilot called inside, and six space-suited figures walked tiredly out. They were not recognizable in their space dress, for even their helmets were too dark to show their faces.

"Gentlemen," the TV announcer said to the survivors, "I'm sure every television set, at the colony and on faraway Earth too, is tuned to this spot. Of course, the big question in all the people's minds is which of the men who were lost are among you alive. Will each of you pass before our camera and give your name?"

Ted felt his nerves tighten as the men, one by one, faced the screen. Two, three, then four bearded men passed and gave their names. Randy's father was not one of them. Two more

The picture flashed on.

to go. Just then the worst possible thing happened. The screen suddenly went gray.

Ted heard Randy groan. The seconds ticked by. Still no picture. Finally, after five minutes, the announcer said that picture service would be restored in a few more minutes. Ted could see the perspiration gleaming on Randy's face, and his fingers were clenching and unclenching continuously.

"What a frightful thing for him to be going through!" Mrs. Kenton whispered to Ted. "I certainly hope and pray his father is one of those remaining two."

The picture flashed on. The announcer spent a moment or two explaining the difficulty that had thrown the picture off; then he called the two remaining men. The fifth showed himself. In the close-up his smiling, grimy face was visible through his helmet.

"Is—that him?" Ted asked tremulously.

Randy's head wagged slowly in the negative. Finally the last man walked up, and Randy gave a scream of joy and sprang over to the screen.

"My name is Robert Matthews," spoke the

bearded man. He smiled and waved into the screen. "Are you listening, Randy boy?"

Ted looked at Randy. His shoulders were hunched over and were shaking with quiet sobs. Ted could see tears of joy in his mother's eyes. Then he realized there was a lump in his own throat.

Randy's father was alive. To Ted, it was almost as though it were his own father who had been found.

CHAPTER FOURTEEN

Peril in the Night

RANDY WOULD HAVE LIKED nothing better than to have been at Lowell Harbor to welcome his father, but the quarantine made that impossible. However, Randy left word for his father to phone him on arrival.

Hours after the sensational telecast, the radio-phone finally buzzed. Randy ran to it, flipped a switch, and listened on the two-way microphone.

"Pops!" Randy exclaimed. "Yes, it's me! How are you?" On and on the excited conversation went.

"Isn't it wonderful, Mom?" Ted said to his mother.

"It certainly is!" she answered. "Your dad and I really believed Randy would never see his father alive again."

Yank had been allowed into the house. He seemed to realize that this was a moment of good times, for he capered about like an animated ball of fur. He even tried to make noises into the mike himself, but Randy playfully pushed him off.

Feeling pretty good himself now, Ted thought that if Yank wanted action he'd give it to him. He cuffed the little animal gently along his head. Yank tore after him, catching him near the air lock. Down went the boy and color bear together. Yank growled menacingly but did not impress Ted with his mock ferocity. Yank got on top of Ted, and Ted called for help.

Just then Randy's long conversation with his father ended, and he came over to join the fun. Then the three of them were scrambling and yelling together. Ted halted his play for a moment to look up and see Jill standing in the doorway, her face beaming as though she would like to join the fun. Mrs. Kenton looked around, and her face darkened.

"You'd better get back in that bed, young lady!" her mother threatened.

Jill squealed and ran off to bed. Ted saw that his mother was not really angry. She was smiling, and Ted knew she was glad to find that Jill was feeling so much better.

The rest of the day passed on the same high note of joy. Where several days ago, everything had been fear and gloom, now everything was rosy. The next day, after Randy had talked with his father again, he was impatient to get out and meet him. Ted, too, was beginning to feel the pinch of the quarantine.

The boys went out to take a look at the garden. The stems were high and full of broad leaves. It looked like a miniature jungle here. And in such a short time! Ted checked the atmosphere gauge that showed the percentage of oxygen to carbon dioxide in the greenhouse. The gas from the carbon dioxide tank had to be just so, or the plants would suffocate from an overabundance of oxygen.

When the boys returned to the living room,

Mrs. Kenton said to them, "I have a surprise for you two. Turn your heads."

They did so, and when she told them to look around they saw a fully dressed Jill standing there, her cheeks pink and healthy again. Ted hugged his sister as though she had been away a long time and was just getting back.

At last, the day that, it had seemed, would never arrive finally did come. Randy was up especially early that morning, saying that he wanted to visit his father before he went to school.

The children were in the living room awaiting breakfast.

"I'm sure they'll let you off from school one more day to be with your father, Randy," Mrs. Kenton called from the kitchen.

"Even if they do, I don't want to lose any time seeing him," Randy said.

Suddenly Jill pointed a shaky finger toward the front door. "L-look, there's a man at the door!"

Ted turned around, startled. "I wonder who . . ." he began.

But Randy was not puzzled. He ran across the

room and flipped the switch that controlled the air lock. A few minutes later a robust man in a space suit entered and pulled off his helmet. He had a rugged, kindly face which showed the effects of the terrible strain he had been under so long. But he was smiling.

"Pops!" Randy cried and threw his arms around him.

"Boy, what a squeeze you have!" Mr. Matthews grunted. "You've grown, Randy."

When their prolonged greeting was over, Randy introduced his father to the Kentons. Ted's hand was almost lost in the large, powerful grip of Mr. Matthews.

"You're just in time for breakfast, Mr. Matthews," Mrs. Kenton said.

"It's been a long time since I've had a home-cooked meal," the man answered wistfully. "I'd like to join you."

As they were eating, Dr. Matthews heard the story of his son's adoption by the Kentons. Then he said, "I can't thank you folks enough for taking care of my boy just as if he were one of your own."

163

"Pops!" Randy cried.

"Randy *has* been one of us," Mrs. Kenton said warmly.

"What do you say about that?" his father asked. "Do you want to leave these nice people?"

Randy looked uncertain. It was a situation he had given little thought to before. "I don't really like leaving them," Randy said hesitantly. Then he seemed to have an idea. "I've got it, Dad! Why can't you come and live here?"

Mr. Matthews laughed. "I'm afraid that's carrying hospitality too far. No, we'll build as a house of our own, as close by as we can. Until we get an allotment of housing material, we'll get a room in headquarters."

"There's no use both of you living there," Mrs. Kenton said. "Why not led Randy stay on here until your house is ready to move into?"

"Sure," Ted put in. "Why can't Randy do that?" He had been saddened at the thought of Randy leaving the household. It had seemed as though Randy was going to be with them always, for he had not believed that Randy's father was ever coming back.

Randy thought this was a fine idea. Ted could

see that he did not like parting with the Kentons any more than they did with him. Mr. Matthews was reluctant to take further advantage of the Kenton hospitality, but at last was talked into the proposition.

The children went along with Randy's father back toward town, following along in the Kenton boat. Mr. Matthews said he'd arrange for Randy to have the day off from school so that the two of them could have a good visit.

The young Kentons were glad to be back in the thick of things. They found school particularly interesting that day, because a field trip was announced by Mr. Garland.

"Every year this class is given an exploring field trip over certain areas of the planet so that you can get a firsthand knowledge of Mars's geography," the instructor declared. "The trip is by plane and will last two days. You must have your parents' consent, of course."

That afternoon, as Ted and Jill left school, Ted said, "What do you think of that trip, Sis?"

"It sounds like fun!" she said. "I hope we can go."

166

"I'd like to, too, but don't forget Mom would be by herself."

"I'd forgotten about that," Jill said disappointedly. "Mother would tell us to go on, if we asked her, I know, but I still wouldn't want to leave her. There are so many things that could happen."

"We'll just have to forget it then," Ted said. "Maybe we can make it another time."

The two kept a brooding silence, and Ted wondered if Jill was as disappointed as he was. When Randy found out that they had decided not to go, he said he did not care to go either.

That night Ted had a dream. In it he was exploring on the great barren desert with Jill and Randy but they wore no helmets and it seemed as though they could hardly get their breath. They gasped and choked, and the dream grew into a nightmare of terror. Suddenly, Ted woke. He sat up in bed in a cold sweat, feeling a strange lightheadedness. His breath was coming hard into his lungs.

It had not only been a dream. Something had happened to the atmosphere in the house.

CHAPTER FIFTEEN

The Peril Continued

R ANDY, WAKE UP!"
Ted was jostling his bedmate. Randy opened sleepy eyes. He seemed to be unaffected by the reduced air pressure in the room. Ted remembered that people vary in their reaction to this.

But when Ted told him of the danger, Randy bounced out of bed with no further prompting. Ted switched on a light, and just as he was reading the air-pressure gauge on the wall, he heard a shrill whistle in the house. It was the air alarm that had gone off automatically. Ted could see that the gauge read dangerously low.

If he and Randy and the others did not get into space suits in a hurry they would suffer serious consequences, one of which could be an attack of the "bends." At worst, they would lose consciousness and die of anoxia—oxygen starvation.

Even before Ted could leave the room to rouse his mother and sister, both were standing at the boys' door.

"We've got to get on space suits right away!" Ted told them. "It looks like all the air pressure in the house is leaking out!"

They went immediately to the closet and began dragging out space dress in a mad flurry of fear. They pulled on the suits and helmets with haste and inflated the airtight outfits with fresh, pressurized oxygen from the small tanks on their backs.

"What do you think has happened to the air drum in the basement?" Mrs. Kenton asked her son over her helmet radio.

"I don't know, but Randy and I can go down there and see," Ted answered.

The boys went downstairs, made a light, and walked over to the giant metal tank recessed in one of the walls. Checking the gauges on the tank, Ted turned to Randy with a frown.

"There's nothing wrong with this," Ted said.

"Then where is the trouble?" Randy asked.

"There must be a leak somewhere in the house," Ted said. "We've got to find out."

The boys went upstairs, and Ted told his mother and sister that all of them should spread out and search the entire house for a leak. There were emergency sealers on hand to plug such a leak when it was found. The sealers were only temporary, but they would last until a full repair could be made by a repairman.

Each of them took a room and worked toward the middle of the house in their search, all lights having been turned on to give maximum illumination. The job was no easy one. Even the slightest crack anywhere would be sufficient to cause the loss of pressure; it was just like a tire tube with a tiny puncture. Ted was the first to finish his assigned area. He had found nothing. Presently Randy was through, then Mrs. Kenton, then Jill. No one had found a leak anywhere, and the entire house had been covered.

"We must have missed it somewhere!" Ted said. "We've wasted a whole hour!"

"The spare cartridges your father told us to have filled!" Randy suddenly exclaimed. "We didn't do it!"

"We forgot to in all the excitement after he left!" Ted groaned.

"What'll we do?" Mrs. Kenton asked, horrified. "In another hour or so, we'll have used up the air in our suits!"

"Can't we refill our suit cartridges from the air drum downstairs?" Jill asked.

Ted shook his head. "It's not built that way."

"Then we must phone for help right away," Mrs. Kenton said and rushed off to the radio-phone.

In a few moments she was back. "They'll send someone from town with spare cartridges right away," she said, "but the man said we couldn't get a repairman until morning to fix the leak. We'll have to stay in our space suits if we don't find the leak."

"Then let's look for it again," Ted suggested.

Once more they spread out all over the house, but this time they changed areas, so that if a mistake had been made before there was less chance of repeating it this time. They renewed their search, and it was not until all were through, again without having found the leak, that they realized that another hour had passed and the man with the spare cartridges had not shown up.

"The gauge in my helmet shows I've got only ten minutes of air left!" Jill said.

The others checked their gauges. All showed

about ten minutes' supply remaining. And there was no guarantee that the spare cartridges would arrive in that time.

Just as Mrs. Kenton was going to the radio-phone to call the air-supply center again, the phone buzzed and she answered it. After listening a moment, she turned to the children with a white face. "The man's boat developed some trouble on the way. He says he can't get here for fifteen minutes."

"That'll be too late!" Jill cried.

Mrs. Kenton relayed this information and then said, "He wants to know if we have any neighbors close by we can borrow from."

"I know it'll take us more than ten minutes to get there and back!" Ted answered, recalling the goodly distance to their closest neighbor.

Mrs. Kenton reported this and then, after listening for several seconds, she finally hung up. "He says that he'll call back to headquarters and get an emergency truck here as quickly as possible. But he can't be certain that it will get here in time either."

Jill began sobbing. Ted could see his mother's

lips trembling, but she was trying to be brave. Mrs. Kenton hugged Jill to her, trying to calm her. Ted saw Randy fidgeting nervously. His own stomach felt queasy, and waves of terror went through him as he thought of the consequences of running out of air.

"Come on, Ted," Randy said finally to his friend, going from the hall into the living room. "We've just got to find that leak. If we can find it and plug it, the house pressure will rise to normal in a couple of minutes. I remember our own place doing that once before!"

"But we've gone over the whole place twice!" Ted argued. "There's no hope!"

"Either we've passed the leak without seeing it," Randy went on, "or the leak is in a spot that we didn't look at."

"But there isn't any place we didn't look!" Ted said. "Of course, there are some places we couldn't get to, like. . . ."

They both thought of it at the same time. Both boys' eyes shifted to the drainage hole in the center of the plastic floor. Here was one spot they had not been able to check. There was a grillwork molded into the plastic that was not easily removable.

"Suppose it is the drain hole, though," Randy said. "How can we find out?"

"I've got it," Ted answered. "We'll plug up the whole thing with a sealer, then check the room gauge to see if the pressure builds up."

A rubberoid sealing patch was taken out of its case and applied over the hole. They flattened it out tightly to assist the adhesive to cling fast

176

in place. Then all four of them went over to the wall to watch the pressure gauge.

A minute passed, and the needle failed to move even the tiniest bit. If this did not work, they knew they would surely be lost, because from where they stood, they could see outside for quite a distance, and still no one was coming.

Over his radio, Ted heard the nervous intake of breath from the others. He knew his hurried breathing must sound the same to them. Actually, fear was hastening their doom because the more scared they were the more oxygen they used up.

Ted stole a look at his helmet gauge. Only three minutes of air remained! His eyes turned to the wall gauge again. He wished he could put out his hand and push it along toward normal. How desperately he wished for it to move!

Ted thought he noticed a flicker of the needle. He blinked his eyes. Yes, it had moved! The others had seen it too.

"It moved!" cried Jill, almost hysterically.

"It certainly did!" her mother burst out. "I saw it!"

The needle continued to climb toward normal. Ted had nothing to say. He was so filled with relief that he was speechless for the moment.

They were all so concerned over the snaillike movement of that all-important needle that they paid no attention to the last few dwindling draughts of air in their suits. Ted was the first to realize that his tank was empty. He began feeling that same lightheadedness he had experienced in his room

"Our suits," he cried out. "Pull them off! The room is just about normal!"

He unclipped his own helmet, then pulled it off and drank in precious gulps of fresh air. The others followed suit. Soon the needle was vertical, indicating that normal pressure and air supply had been restored.

It was five minutes before a light came swiftly across the desert, moving in their direction. They heard the pop of an exhaust a moment later as a big-wheeled truck pulled up to a roaring stop outside.

Ted knew it must be the arrival of the emergency cartridges. But they had been five minutes late. A shudder shook him as he realized what a close call this had been. Had they not found the leak when they did, none of them in the house would now be alive to greet the men.

CHAPTER SIXTEEN

Disappointment

THE NEXT AFTERNOON, when Ted, Jill, and Randy arrived home from school, Mrs. Kenton told them that the repairmen had taken care of the leak in the drain. It seemed that the hole had been partially stopped up so that the water had collected and frozen in it, causing the pipe to crack.

Jill had been impatient to talk ever since she had gotten in the house. Now her chance had come. "Mother, you know what Mr. Garland wants us to do?" she asked eagerly.

Mrs. Kenton smiled. "What does he want you to do?" she asked.

"He wants us to bring Yank to school for a demonstration lesson in Martian zoology," Ted broke in.

Jill's face clouded over with disappointment. "I wanted to tell her," she muttered.

"Sorry!" Ted said. "I didn't know it was a secret."

Jill slapped at him playfully, but Ted ducked in time.

"You little clowns stop performing and get ready for supper," Mrs. Kenton said. "We're eating early because I have a surprise for you."

"A surprise!" Jill echoed. "What is it?"

Her mother smiled secretly but did not answer. Jill ran off to her room and the boys went to theirs. When the children had dressed and washed, they seated themselves at the dining-room table. Mrs. Kenton brought in a large platter of real roast beef.

"This is the surprise!" Jill said.

"If it isn't, I'll settle for it!" Ted put in.

Beef was a rarity on Martian tables. It was brought in only occasionally on the rocket supply ships. Most meat was of the dehydrated and cube variety that took less space.

"No, this is not the surprise I was talking about," Mrs. Kenton said, "although it was to me when the supply boat drove up this morning with special rations."

"Do you mean there is still another?" Jill asked.

Her mother nodded and went on. "The beef took only a few minutes to roast in the electronic oven. I remember my grandmother making so much of a pressure cooker. She probably would never have believed there would be an oven of the future that cooked in even less time than the pressure cooker and without any heat whatsoever."

When the main course of the meal was over and apple pie was brought in, the children were sure this was the surprise Mrs. Kenton had promised. She said the supply boat had brought the fresh apples with the meat. But even the treat of apple pie was not the special surprise.

When supper was over Mrs. Kenton conducted the children into the living room and had them gather around a recording machine owned by their father. Mrs. Kenton set a spool of wire rotating and told them to listen.

"Hello, kids!" came a voice.

"Father!" Jill exclaimed.

They listened to a message addressed especially to them. When it was over, Mrs. Kenton explained that their father had called by remote broadcast from his distant work during the day. Then he had had her make a special wire recording for them so that they could hear it later. Mrs. Kenton told them this was the surprise. The children admitted that this was an even greater one than the beef and the apple pie.

"I thought Father sounded sort of sad or disappointed," Jill commented.

"You were right, dear," Mrs. Kenton replied. "Their work hasn't gone along as well as they expected. They had a small landslide that buried the best of their diggings, which will take larger machinery than they've got to unearth. On top of that, the tracks they thought would prove to be a clue to the disappearing Martians aren't human at all but belong to a group of animals they have already classified."

"Gee!" Ted murmured sympathetically, remembering how enthusiastic his father had been before he had left. Now the greatest mystery on Mars—that of the disappearing Martians —was just as baffling as before.

"Because of this," Mrs. Kenton said, "they're ending the expedition ahead of time and coming home."

"That's why he said he'd be seeing us shortly," Randy said.

"I'm glad to hear that, anyway," Jill murmured.

"When will he be back?" Ted asked.

"Within two or three days, he said," his mother replied.

"That will be before the class goes on the. . . ." Jill burst out, then covered her mouth with her hand as she caught herself.

"Before the class goes on what?" Mrs. Kenton asked.

"We'll have to tell her now," Jill said lamely to the boys.

"The class is going on a sight-seeing rocket-plane tour of Mars next week," Ted explained.

His mother looked at Jill curiously. "But why such a secret about it?"

"We just thought you wouldn't be especially interested," Jill said, "since we weren't going."

"Don't you want to?" Mrs. Kenton asked.

"Oh, yes!" Jill said. "Only. . . ."

A knowing look came into Mrs. Kenton's eyes. "I see! You didn't tell me about it and show your interest because you didn't want to leave me here alone! That's it, isn't it?"

Mrs. Kenton threw an arm around each of her children. "That was a very unselfish thing for you to do," she said. "But now that Father will be back sooner than he expected, you'll be able to go after all."

"Can we really, Mother?" Jill asked enthusiastically, her eyes full of stars.

"Will it be dangerous?" Mrs. Kenton asked cautiously.

"There have been lots of these trips made already," Randy volunteered. "There hasn't been any trouble yet."

186

"Well, you have my permission," Mrs. Kenton said, "but your Father will have to agree too."

"But tomorrow's the last day we can make reservations!" Jill protested. "If we wait until he comes, we can't make it!"

"Go ahead and make your reservations then," her mother said. "I don't believe your father will object if I don't. But if he does, you can cancel your seats."

"We'll lose our money if we do that," Ted said, "but I guess that can't be helped." Suddenly Ted looked fearful. "Dad did leave the checkbook, didn't he?"

"Yes, he left it," his mother assured him with a smile.

"Pops is coming out here tonight for a visit," Randy said. "Now that you and Jill are going on the trip, Ted, I think I'll ask Pops to let me go along too!"

"That'll be great!" Ted said. "All three of us will go together."

The next morning the children got Yank up at an early hour so that he could go off to school with them.

"You'd better be on your good behavior to-day," Jill warned the color bear as they climbed into the boat. "If you cut up like you do in the house, Mr. Garland may flunk us!"

Yank looked at her solemnly as though he understood. But then his broad mouth widened in a grin as if he were telling the girl that he had no intention of taking her remarks seriously! As soon as the boat moved down the waterway, Yank stood up.

"Sit down, Yank," Randy told him. "You're rocking the boat!"

Yank paid no attention to this reproof. He was enjoying himself.

"Stop him!" Jill squealed. "He'll turn us over!"

Randy rose unsteadily to his feet and moved toward the rear. He made a lurch at him, but Yank leaned out of his reach and looked back, grinning merrily.

"You naughty bear!" Jill cried, half in fear and half in anger.

Randy leaned forward again and pulled Yank back on top of himself with a fierce jerk. As

188

Yank went over the side with a splash.

Randy went down, the bear rolled off him and up on the edge of the boat.

Randy lunged at him, but Yank's fur slipped from the boy's fingers. Yank went over the side with a splash into the frigid water. As soon as Yank touched the water, Randy made a grab at him and caught one of his forepaws. Yank screeched in shock and fear at the sudden freezing plunge.

Ted slowed the boat down and turned the wheel over to Jill while he helped Randy pull the Martian animal aboard again. Yank looked thoroughly beaten as he flopped, dripping and cold, into the bottom of the boat. His round little ears were drooping sadly, and the corners of his mouth were turned down. He looked more like a polar bear now, because crystals of frost were growing all over him.

In spite of themselves, the children had to laugh at their little pet's predicament. As the shiny spikes of frost popped out on his face, Yank would brush at them furiously with his paws. Even his eyebrows were growing icy. This further increased the laughter of the children.

"I guess that'll teach you to behave, Yank!" Ted chuckled, and offered to take the wheel back.

"Let me drive the rest of the way," Jill said.

Ted yielded to her, and he was pleased at the skill with which she drove and docked at the science building.

The children were a little ahead of time, and this gave them a chance before class to tell Mr. Garland about their wish to make the trip with the others. Randy had gotten his father's permission the night before.

Mr. Garland frowned as he looked over his list, and Ted had a sinking feeling.

The teacher looked up. "Two of you can go, but not all three, I'm afraid. Yesterday I thought that quite a few more could go, but I found out last night I had omitted several names from my list. Which one of you wants to drop out?"

CHAPTER SEVENTEEN

Yank in School

A T THIS SURPRISING REMARK from their teacher, the young folks' faces drooped with disappointment. For several seconds none of the three had anything to say. Mr. Garland idly fingered the two checks they had handed him.

Finally Randy spoke up. "I'll drop out," he said. "I've been on a trip like this before with my father, but Ted and Jill haven't."

"That's a fine decision, Randy," Mr. Garland said. He handed one of the checks back and added the Kenton children's names to his list.

For the moment, all interest in the trip was gone for Ted. He knew Randy must be keenly disappointed. Although until late yesterday none of them had expected to go, they had talked a long time last night with Mr. Matthews over the exciting things they would see. Randy had been quite as interested as Ted and Jill about the coming adventure.

Suddenly Ted said: "Take Jill's and my name off the list too, Mr. Garland. I don't think two of us should go if the third one can't."

"That's right," Jill agreed.

"That doesn't make sense, you two," Randy protested.

Mr. Garland looked up. "There's no sense both of you missing the trip for the sake of one. It's the educational opportunity of a lifetime."

Ted then gave in, although he knew it was not going to be nearly so much fun without Randy along.

The discussion ended abruptly when Ted heard a shriek from one of the incoming pupils. He turned and was shocked to see Yank chasing one of the girls toward the back of the room.

"Yank, come back here!" Jill called, when she saw what was going on.

But Yank was once more enjoying himself. He was grunting happily as he pursued the girl around the back of the room, and along the side toward the front. The bear's three owners caught the little fellow as he was coming around again.

"I just patted him and he took out after me!" gasped the girl who had been chased.

"He was just playing," Ted told her. "He couldn't hurt you if he tried. His teeth are only made for chewing soft flowers."

Mr. Garland restored order and announced that zoology would be the first subject of the day so that the active Yank could then be taken outside. First Mr. Garland stood Yank on the platform at the head of the class with Ted to help keep him still.

The teacher pointed out the physical characteristics of the Martian animal, touching Yank's paws, head, jaws, and other parts with a pointer. Yank followed the movement of the stick with his eyes. Then the whole class started giggling. The bear was looking at the stick cross-eyed.

Ted had to force down a grin. He could see

that Mr. Garland was having the same trouble. When Yank got tired of following the stick with his eyes, he seized it in his mouth and began gnawing on it. This brought a burst of laughter from the pupils.

Ted took the stick from Yank, and the bear thought this was a signal for them to wrestle. At home, this was the way Ted usually got him to play.

"Get off me, Yank," Ted muttered in a low, angry voice. "We're at school, not home! I thought we warned you to behave yourself here! You're just trying to show off!"

Yank seemed to get the tone of Ted's outburst, even if he could not understand the words. He stopped his foolishness and actually kept as still as a little gentleman for the next few minutes as Mr. Garland continued to demonstrate.

But then he could hold off no longer. As the instructor was leaning over close to him to point out the peculiar upsweep of his blue-tipped eyebrows, Yank's big red tongue came out of his mouth and scraped along Mr. Garland's cheek.

The teacher blushed at the renewed laughter

as he wiped his face with his handkerchief. Ted was worried lest Mr. Garland hold Yank's behavior against him. But the teacher was a good sport and said, with a grin, "You win, Yank. Better take him outside, Ted. This will have to conclude our study of Martian color bears for a while!"

Ted took Yank outside and tied him beneath the classroom window so that he could watch him every now and then. Ted knew what the animal must be thinking: "Please let me in! I'll behave myself."

When Ted returned, the class was quiet again. Mr. Garland set up the projector for a color movie on American history. But this was not merely a history lesson. The children were told to study the costumes and architecture. It was actually several studies in one.

When the picture was over an hour later, Ted was blinking his eyes to accommodate them to the harsh daylight again when one of the children cried out, "Look!"

Every eye in the room did look. Following the pointing finger, they turned their gaze to one of the transparent side walls. There was Yank standing with his button nose pressed flat against the plastic, just like a small child looking out a glass window. This brought another round of laughter from the class. On this note, Mr. Garland dismissed the class for lunch.

That afternoon, as Ted, Jill, and Randy were about to leave for the day, Mr. Garland called them back just as they reached the door.

"Oh-oh," Ted murmured with dread. "He's going to give it to us now for bringing that little cutup to school!"

Meekly the three of them stood in front of the teacher's desk. He looked up at them and smiled. "I don't think that little bit of fun hurt us this morning. But please don't bring Yank back again! I'm afraid one day of him is all I can stand." He looked outside where they could see Yank seated on the ground.

He smiled again, and the relieved children grinned back. They had started toward the door, when Ted, who was looking back, pulled Randy and Jill to a stop.

"Listen," he said. He turned them around and

197

they heard part of a conversation Mr. Garland was having with one of the other pupils that might very well work to their benefit.

"Did I hear that boy say he couldn't make the trip?" Jill whispered excitedly.

"I thought he did," Ted replied.

They waited expectantly, hoping that the teacher would look up and call them back. Ted felt a new surge of hope rise in him when Mr. Garland finally motioned to them. The boy, meanwhile, had left.

"I've just had a cancellation," Mr. Garland told them. "Randy, you can make that trip after all, if you want to."

"Do I?" Randy burst out, his face beaming. He fumbled around in his pocket for the check his father had given him. Then he pulled out the rumpled slip of paper.

The instructor smoothed it out and wrote Randy's name on the list. The children left the room and walked happily down the hall.

"That was a swell thing you did, Randy," Jill said, "giving up your place to one of us. I'm so glad that you really can go!"

198

"Please don't bring Yank back."

"I'm glad too," Randy admitted. "After all we talked about last night, I sure wanted to go badly!"

Yank hopped around excitedly as he saw his friends coming up to release him.

"You'll never see this place again, Yank," Ted said to him sternly, as he untied him. "I guess you're just not cut out to be a school pupil."

For this remark, Ted got a juicy lick on the side of his helmet.

CHAPTER EIGHTEEN

Trouble in the Air

D R. KENTON ARRIVED home the following afternoon. Ted could see that he was a very different person from the one who had set out. His father looked tired and beaten. Even the special meal of fresh fruits and vegetables from their garden failed to interest him very much.

As they were eating supper, his wife asked him, "Why was this expedition so important to you, John?"

"I suppose I had counted too much on its being a huge success," the scientist replied. "Then too, I thought it would solve that all-important question of the disappearing ancient

201

Martians that's been puzzling us ever since the first landing was made here ten years ago."

"There'll be other expeditions," Mrs. Kenton said encouragingly. "Some day you'll find the answer, I'm sure."

"Yes, I suppose so," Dr. Kenton said. But Ted could see that his father was very downcast because of the expedition's failure.

"I wish I had known you were coming when you did," Mrs. Kenton said to her husband. "I would have invited Mr. Matthews to eat with us. You knew that Randy had found his father, didn't you?"

Ted was glad to see his father smile as he turned to Randy. "Yes, we got the news," Dr. Kenton said. "I'm sure glad for you, Randy. You see, it never pays to give up hope. I'll be pleased to meet your father."

Just then Yank came bounding in from the living room. The bear had taken to the taste of lettuce leaves, and Ted would occasionally slip him a leaf from the table. Yank sidled up to Ted, where he sat next to his father, eyeing the crisp leaves on the boy's plate. Yank's other eye was cast warily at Dr. Kenton, whom he still appeared not to regard as a close friend.

"When are you and I going to be friends, Yank?" the scientist said as Ted handed the bear a green leaf. He reached out to pet the little Martian animal, but Yank drew back. "I can't understand your attitude, young fellow."

Ted thought this the proper moment to bring up a very important matter. "Dad," he began, "Jill and Randy and I have signed up for a sight-seeing plane tour of Mars with our school class. Mom says it's all right for us to go if you agree."

Dr. Kenton thought a moment, and Ted felt doubtful. Then his father said, "I think it would be a grand thing for you. You can get a lot better picture of this planet from the air than you ever can from the ground."

"Goody, we can go!" Jill cried out.

Ted felt like shouting himself, for now the last barrier had been removed and they were going for sure.

The next week found twenty-five eager students stepping into a sleek jet craft from the roll-away ladder at Lowell Harbor. Randy and Ted found a double seat together, and Jill sat with a girl friend. When all the passengers were in, Mr. Garland said that they could remove their space helmets.

When all were seated, they waved to their parents and relatives who stood on the ground.

"I'm as excited as if I'd never made a trip like this!" Randy said.

"I'm excited too!" Ted admitted. He didn't add that he had scarcely slept the night before because he was in such a dither of anticipation.

Mr. Garland told the children to fasten their safety belts, as they were almost ready to take off. In a few minutes they felt the ship moving beneath them. Ted waved a final farewell to his parents and Mr. Matthews, for he had a seat beside the window. When they waved back, Ted felt a little uneasy. It was the first time he had ever been away from his folks. He wondered fearfully if something would happen on the flight so that he would never see them again.

Swiftly the rocket plane picked up speed.

Then, with a whoosh of jets, it launched itself into the air.

"We're off!" one of the boys shouted gaily.

Soon Lowell Harbor was only a small circle in the red desert behind them, and the vast stretches of wilderness began to come into view. Mr. Garland pointed out the important natural formations as they cruised along. By now almost all of Mars had been accurately mapped. There were miles and miles of wind-ribbed sand dunes with rows of furrows like a farmer's carefully seeded fields.

Ted had never before realized the wonder of the canals until he saw them from this height. They were straight as arrows, and some were tremendous in size, even dwarfing the majesty of the Grand Canyon of Arizona. It caused him to wonder again about those very accomplished engineers of the ancient past who had built them and had since so mysteriously disappeared.

Ted recognized much of the landscape from their geography study. Some of the ocher-red deserts and forests had been named far back in the past before the twenty-first century. They passed over the great oasis of Solis Lacus and the dense woodland of Mare Sirenum. But always there were canals, and more canals, draining the great icecaps and supplying the entire planet.

"Isn't the sky pretty?" Jill said to Ted and Randy who were sitting behind her. "It seems we're closer to the stars when we're off the ground."

Ted had to agree with her. The heavens were a deep gorgeous violet, with the starlight pulsing softly through. They traced the slow movement of Phobos, the timeteller, and they could also pick out the distant tiny moon, Deimos, that resembled a white arc light.

The hours passed all too quickly for the eager sight-seers.

"We're over the Great Martian Forest," Mr. Garland told them late that afternoon. "It's the end of the line. After we've covered this, we'll start back."

Ted looked groundward, seeing what resembled a colossal, sprawling beast spread out in all directions. Ted shuddered at the sight. Many explorers had been trapped in this terrible wilderness and had never come out alive. Wild animals, blind trails, and carnivorous whip plants were thought to have destroyed them.

Suddenly someone called out as he pointed down, "Look, what's that moving?"

All stared where he pointed. In an open space inside the forest, numerous creatures were rolling along like a tide.

"They're blue rovers," Mr. Garland said. "They're something like the old American bison that roamed the plains of the United States."

More strange animals were seen, and still the plane was not out of the huge forest. If anything, the jungle grew even more densely, and now rocky cliffs and shallow gorges could be seen among the thick vegetation. Mars had no extremely deep or high natural formations such as the Earth had.

"Most of the forest turns brown in the winter," Mr. Garland addressed his students, "but when the polar cap melts in the spring, everything pops out green again."

Ted knew that the seasons were twice as long

on Mars as they were on Earth, even though the days and nights were just about the same. How frightfully cold must be the winters, he thought. But on the other hand, what a long, nice summer to enjoy!

Finally the dense growth began thinning out again as the outer fringe of the forest was reached. Suddenly, without warning, the plane careened sharply on its side. Some of the students were flung out of their seats, and they screamed in terror. Mr. Garland, who had been standing by a window, was thrown backward onto the floor. When the ship had righted itself, Mr. Garland climbed slowly to his feet.

"Anybody hurt?" the teacher asked.

No one else appeared to be, but Ted saw Mr. Garland grimace in pain. He seemed to have injured his ankle.

"Mr. Garland, *you're* hurt!" Ted said.

"Never mind me!" the instructor said. "Put your safety belts on—quickly!"

His students did so, and then the plane started bucking again. Poor Mr. Garland was flung against the wall this time, but he recovered himself and hobbled into the pilot's cabin to see what was wrong. Ted heard his classmates babbling in fright all around him. He and Randy tried to quiet Jill's mounting terror.

"Take it easy," Ted said to her. "It may not be anything serious."

Mr. Garland was back in a few minutes, and Ted could see that his face was grave.

"We've got to bail out, kids," he told the class grimly.

"Into *that?*" cried one of the boys, pointing to the forest below.

"We've no other choice, the pilot tells me," Mr. Garland replied, his voice shaky. "There's a fire in the jets, and we can't crash-land without wrecking the plane."

Terrified, the students stared at him, as though they still could not believe what he was saying.

"He says there's an open space ahead of us where we can parachute down," Mr. Garland went on. "He's sending a message for help now.

209

We've got enough supplies and air to last us until a search party comes from Lowell Harbor. There's no cause for alarm."

There was no more time for talk. Despite his obviously painful injury, the teacher quickly distributed chutes and showed the children how to put them on. The chutes were specially designed for use in Mars's rare atmosphere. Next, space helmets were donned. Then Mr. Garland lined the children up with their rip cords fastened to an overhead cord for automatic opening of the chutes when they jumped. Ted, his sister, and Randy had stayed together, and they found themselves the first three in line to jump.

Chutes with supplies had been shoved out first by hand, and then Mr. Garland signaled to Ted for the first jump. Things had moved so swiftly that Ted hardly had time to become scared. Randy and Jill seemed to feel the same way. The ship was still jerking erratically and plumes of smoke swirled about. The oval door was open, and Ted saw yawning space beneath him. At Mr. Garland's word, he took a deep breath and sprang out. He felt the straps on his

Down, down he went.

back yank him sharply as the chute popped open.

Down, down he went. Finally he glanced upward and saw two other parachutes above him. They would be Jill and Randy, he thought. He looked groundward again to see where he was heading. Just as Mr. Garland had said, a flat open space lay beneath.

Once more he glanced upward. There were still only two other chutes above. Where were the others? Hadn't they jumped too? Then he spied the ship at a considerable distance away. It was careening downward as though heading for a crash!

Ted felt a sick tug in his stomach. It looked as though the three of them were the only ones who were going to escape alive. The ship must have gone out of control before the others could jump!

CHAPTER NINETEEN

Terror in the Night

A s soon as Ted reached the ground, he made for the spot where he had seen the supply chutes land. If these were lost, especially the one with the spare air cartridges, Randy and Jill and he could never survive until help came.

Ted ran down a dusty ravine. His eyes searched clumps of bushes and spiky cactus, and a momentary panic came over him. The chutes were not in sight. Just then he was aware that a strong wind was blowing. The chutes had probably carried farther than he had thought. He searched some more, and his heart quickened with joy when he found the two parachutes within yards of each other, half buried in the sand beyond a big boulder.

As soon as he had found these, he thought immediately of Randy and Jill. He should have seen them by now. He returned to the spot where he had come down, but they were nowhere around. A new terror crept into his breast. Could the wind have carried them farther up into the forest, possibly into the dangerous part where the brush grew dense as jungle and deadly whip plants thrived? The wind was stronger than ever now, but he ducked into it and renewed his search.

He made a thorough examination of the territory all around, but after a half hour's time he still had not located Jill and Randy. For the sixth time he returned to his original spot where he had left the parachutes of supplies. By now the blood red of approaching sunset was filling the sky, and grotesque shadows were creeping over the ground.

Ted could not remember when he had felt any more depressed and lonely than he did at this moment. He could imagine all sorts of terrible things happening to his sister and friend. By now, the wind had died down. Thank goodness the blow had not brought on one of those violent dust storms, he thought.

Suddenly he heard a noise overhead that quickened hope in him. It had sounded like the drone of a plane! He leaped to his feet from where he had been slumped on the ground and searched the darkening starry sky. Yes, there was a plane! He could hardly believe it when he saw that the number on the wedge-shaped wing was the same as that of the ship from which he had bailed out. That meant that the plane had not crashed after all!

As the plane roared overhead, he ran back and forth and waved his hands frantically to get the attention of someone in it. To his dismay the plane kept on going and presently was lost in the approaching twilight.

He thought the world had ended for him now. Jill and Randy were gone, and hopes of rescue too. But then he heard a crashing of bushes near by. His heart thudded against his ribs in fear. He was remembering that wild animals inhabited this district, and he was totally unarmed.

Then he heard his name called. A moment later Randy and Jill came running up! He was never so glad to see two people in his life as he was then.

"What happened to you?" he asked them.

"The wind carried us down into the forest a little way," Jill answered. "Oh, Ted, I was scared to death! Those whip plants throw out arms like an octopus at anything that comes near them! I almost got caught by one!"

Ted showed them the chutes that held spare air cartridges and food. Unfortunately, Mr. Garland had thrown out only a few supply chutes, not all of them.

They had never eaten with space helmets on, but they had learned about the tiny air-lock opening in the facepiece of the helmet that made this possible.

"These will last us through the night," Ted said. "I don't know what we'll do after that. A search party probably won't get here that quick."

Just then Jill heard the plane returning. Ted hurriedly explained that this was the one they had been on and that it had not crashed after all. He said that all three of them should run back and forth and wave like everything to try to attract their attention this time.

Ted thought that the plane had missed them again, but then he saw it bank and head back toward them. The ship circled overhead for several minutes, and the children saw a parachute drop out. They followed the chute to the ground with their eyes and ran over to it.

"Here's a note," Ted said, untying an envelope from the chute. He opened it. "It says: 'Open the long case and you will find a walkie-talkie radio in it. Turn it on, and we'll speak with you.'"

They did this. Then Ted spoke into the mike, "Can you hear me?"

"Yes," came Mr. Garland's voice. "We had just above given up hope of sighting you. The ship went out of control just after you three jumped. But the fire in the engine burned out soon after, and the pilot regained control. We should be able to get back to Lowell Harbor all right, even though we're crippled. Are you three hurt?"

"No, sir, just scared," Ted answered.

"We'll send you down all the rest of our air cartridges and more food and water," the teacher went on. "They'll last you through tomorrow, and by that time a search party should be back in a helicopter. We can't possibly land, ourselves, because of the terrain and our damaged engine. I'd come down myself to stay with you, but my ankle is broken and I'm afraid I wouldn't be much help. However, if you want me to. . . ."

"I think we'll be all right," Ted said bravely, yet feeling an encroaching dread even as he said it.

"There's an electron rifle and flashlights in with the other stuff," Mr. Garland said. "I don't think anything will bother you, though; otherwise I wouldn't leave you alone. Most of the animals stay back in the thickest part of the forest."

"Will you be going now?" Ted asked.

"Yes, there's no way else we can help you except send rescuers as quickly as possible," Mr.

Garland declared. "Whatever you do, don't leave that spot."

That ended their conversation. Presently the other supply chutes filled the air, and Randy and the two young Kentons retrieved them. Then, lonesomely, the three watched the plane disappear into the sunset.

"I'm afraid," Jill murmured, casting an anxious glance around her at the forbidding woodland.

"I am too, Sis," Ted confessed. He looked at Randy, and his eyes were enough to tell that he was frightened too.

They looked around for some place of protection overnight. As the sun disappeared behind a distant ridge, they found a shallow opening under a clump of rocks that would shield them on three sides at least. Then they ate from a food packet, and after this they admitted that they felt better.

"If we get through this night safely," Ted said, "we'll probably make it all right."

At last darkness set in. Phobos was making one of his frequent trips across the heavens, but his light was weaker than moonglow on Earth. However, it seemed to Ted that it wasn't quite so lonely now, with the sky burning with its millions of cold lights. Yet it was still frightening to know that the three of them were off by themselves in probably the most perilous region of Mars.

They decided it was best not to use their flashlights unnecessarily, lest they attract wild beasts. They kept the atomic rifle handy in case it was needed in a hurry. Ted suggested that two of them sleep while one stood watch. Jill said she'd like to take the first watch because she was too nervous to sleep anyhow.

Ted was just about to doze off some minutes later when Jill's scream blasted into his radio and brought him springing to his feet.

"There!" Jill said, pointing.

Randy too was wide awake now, and the three of them stared, fear-stricken, across the dark drifts at a giant creature which stood at a distance looking at them. The light of Phobos and the stars was bright enough to show his awesome outline.

"What is it?" Ted whispered to Randy.

"It's an elephant ant," Randy whispered softly. "See that trunklike sucker on its head? Get the gun, Ted. These things are mean."

Ted caught up the atomic rifle and set it for fire, thinking all the while how Mr. Garland had missed his guess about their not being troubled by animals. Slowly the enormous insect approached the opening in the rocks. It was indeed the height of an elephant. Ted could hear the rustle of its hard-shelled body as it walked nearer.

The Martian animal's slowness up until now deceived Ted, for, without warning, the insect broke into a rapid run. Bravely Ted tried to take careful aim and protect the two unarmed ones with him. But even as he fired the gun, Jill bumped him in her mad dash to escape the oncoming horror.

Ted saw a blinding glare that lit up the scene for a moment as brightly as noonday. In that shocking instant Ted got a vivid view of the elephant ant, its brown spindly legs and antenna shining glossily, its curling trunk out-thrust at them menacingly. But as the blast of the rifle died out and the ant continued to charge, Ted knew he had missed his mark.

There was no time to fire again. Ted couldn't carry much, but he dropped his useless weapon and gathered up the spare air cartridges. Then swiftly he darted after Jill and Randy, who seemed to have found a way of escape. He saw

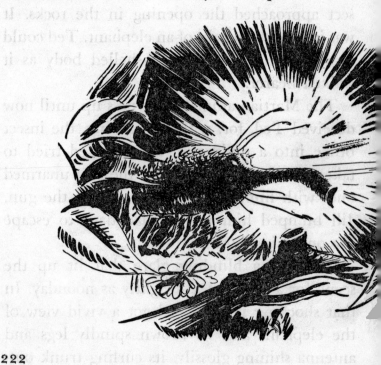

them disappearing through a narrow passage beside the rock. He was glad to see that Randy had managed to hang onto one of the flashlights and was leading the way with it.

Ted didn't know how long they ran up and down rocky inclines and gullies. But they seemed to be leaving their enemy behind. They ducked in and out of clutching vines and creepers. More than once, Ted dropped one of the bulky

air tanks, but he retrieved them, for they were the most precious things they possessed. Finally he caught up with Randy.

"Help me take these!" he urged Randy.

The boy took some and they hurried on after Jill, whose fear seemed to have given her unusual speed. At last they reached the point where they could punish themselves no longer. Jill had fallen exhausted to the ground, and Ted felt as if he were ready to drop too. If the ant reached them now, it simply couldn't be helped. Ted had sacrificed the rifle for the precious air cartridges, but he was not sorry he had done so.

They sprawled breathlessly on the ground, their chests heaving, their eyes staring fearfully in the direction they had come. Any instant they expected to see the horrible creature bearing down on them again. But after several minutes, during which time the animal had not appeared, Ted felt they had eluded it. For the first time since the terrifying adventure, he felt that he could relax.

And yet he could not relax, really, even now. For the balance of the night still lay before them.

CHAPTER TWENTY

Lost Underground

THE THREE OF THEM decided it was not safe to go back to the open area tonight. After waiting a while longer still in the dark to see that their attacker was not coming, they searched the gloom around for a place to spend the rest of the night.

Randy found an opening in the dense underbrush ahead of them. Jill and Ted followed him and his flashlight beam along the trail. Suddenly they saw him stop dead in his tracks. Ted walked abreast of him.

"What do you see?" Ted asked.

Randy did not reply but instead shot his light

225

ahead into the darkness. Ted saw before them a huge cave entrance.

"Gosh, do you suppose that's the den of some wild animal?" Ted asked.

"I don't know," Randy answered in a quivery voice. "It seems like a good place to stay if it isn't."

Jill had joined them by now. She too had taken some of the load of the spare oxygen cartridges.

"Are we going into that spooky place?" Jill asked.

"We can go up to it carefully and shine our light in," Ted said. "But we'd better be ready to run if something comes charging out! I wish I had that gun now!"

Jill hung back as Randy and Ted moved stealthily forward toward the black cavern entrance. Randy had his light shining directly into it all the time they were moving. When they were at the threshold of the cave, they got a good view of the interior.

"It's not deep at all!" Ted said. "It just goes back a little way."

"It looks deserted too," Randy added. "Seems safe to me. What do you think, Ted?"

"Let's go inside and see if there's anything lying around," Ted suggested. "If it's a den, there ought to be bones and things."

Cautiously they entered the cavern. Its ceiling reached high over their heads and the opening was festooned with trailing vines and creepers. Even the jungle growth seemed to have taken over, weeds and thick grass choking the floor. Boulders of all sizes were scattered around.

"It looks like it hasn't been used for years and years," Ted commented.

They flashed the light over the whole interior, but there was no sign of recent use. There was one other exit—a narrow passage at the rear.

"If we close up that rear opening with a big stone, it ought to be safe for us to stay here," Randy said.

Ted agreed with him. They called Jill, and the three shoved a large red boulder in front of the narrow passage. They divided watches again, but before relaxing for the night, they replaced their air cartridges with new ones.

Randy took first watch this time. Ted was very tired from their exhausting race and had trouble falling asleep, but the next thing he knew, Randy was shaking him to change watch.

The rest of the night passed without further disturbance. The boys got softhearted about calling on Jill for her turn, and rather than wake her, they stood her duty. Another change of air cylinders had to be made before morning. Ted was able to change Jill's while she slept.

The orange glow of dawn was a welcome sight to the children. Things did not seem half so grim in the dawn as they had the night before. The sun's feeble rays shone directly into the cave mouth. The boulder covering the rear opening was still in place.

Ted caught Randy's eyes staring thoughtfully at the boulder. He wondered if Randy was thinking the same thing that he was: *What was on the other side of that mysterious opening?*

"Hadn't we better be getting back to the open place?" Jill asked, as they were putting on fresh air tanks again.

"The search party won't be coming until a few hours yet," Randy said. "Besides, it's not very far."

Ted knew then that Randy, too, was curious about the opening. He was stalling their return.

Ted then came right out with it. "I'd sure like to know what's on the other side of that rock."

"Why don't we go and see?" Randy said eagerly.

"We could go just a little way," Ted added, glancing at Jill, whose face showed doubt. "Just a few feet even."

Jill gave in grudgingly, but she got the boys to promise that they wouldn't go far. "Don't forget, we've got some food back there," she reminded them, "and I'm getting hungry."

They left the air cartridges in the cave and walked through the enticing opening, Ted in the lead. He flicked on his flashlight, for it was pitch dark. Ahead of him he saw a narrow passageway. Slowly he moved along it, Randy and Jill right behind him.

They were completely unprepared for the

They felt themselves tumbling downward.

shock that next came to them. Suddenly the ground dropped away under their feet, and they felt themselves tumbling downward!

All three of them cried out in terror as they fell. Finally Ted felt his body striking a cushioned surface. Then he was rolling down an incline of the same soft material. Down, down, head over heels he went—deeper and deeper into the core of the red planet, it seemed.

At last his body stopped turning. Something crashed into him from behind. Then he heard heavy breathing and gasping and he knew that it was either Randy or Jill who had collided with him.

"Jill? Randy?" he asked in a shuddery voice, still dazed by their rough experience.

"Yes," Randy's voice came weakly.

"Jill!" Ted cried. "Where are you?"

"Here I am," she answered, from a few feet away. "What happened to us?"

"I don't know," her brother answered dully. He felt around for broken bones, but he appeared to be uninjured.

"Are you two all right?" he asked Jill and Randy.

They said they thought so. By now Ted could see their forms very faintly. There was light coming from somewhere. Their next task was to try to find a way out of this dismal place.

"I knew we should have gone back!" Jill complained bitterly. "Now we probably never will!"

"I'm sorry, Sis," Ted said lamely. "You were right. I'm sure glad we changed our air tanks before we left!"

"Let's start looking for a way to the top," Randy said. "The search party will never find us down here."

They discovered that the flashlight had been smashed in the fall. They would have to depend now on catlike vision to show them the way. As nearly as Ted could make out, they were still in a corridor. It stretched mysteriously ahead of them, turning a bend about fifty feet away.

"That seems to be the only way we can go," Ted said, looking forward. "We certainly can't climb back up the way we came down." He looked behind at the steep, rugged incline they had so unexpectedly tumbled down. The slope was covered with a matting of lichens or moss that had broken their fall.

They walked along the corridor. Finally the light at the far end began to get brighter.

"It looks like daylight ahead!" Jill said hopefully.

They increased their pace in the hope of finding a way leading back to the surface of the ground. They made a final turn in the winding underground aisle. Then the corridor abruptly blossomed into a mammoth open area, still underground.

The sight that faced them quickened their heartbeats and made their mouths sag open in amazement. Before them stood a towering iron gate, through which they could see evidence of one-time human habitation!

"What in the world have we found?" Ted exclaimed.

"It must be a city!" Randy burst out. "It is! We've found an underground Martian city!"

233

CHAPTER TWENTY-ONE

A Struggle Against Time

A MARTIAN CITY!" Ted echoed. "Wouldn't Dad like to be in on this!"

"I don't care about an old city!" Jill complained. "I just want to get out of here!"

"Maybe we can find a way to the top from in there," Ted proposed. "There's no other place we can go."

The three walked up to the towering gates and began tugging on them. At first the gates would not budge, but after much struggling, the children got one open wide enough on its creaking hinges so that they could squeeze through. Once inside, they began walking along a rocky avenue lined with small buildings and statues. The high dome of the city gleamed with a light of its own, illuminating the entire grand underground area like brilliant moonlight.

"The glow has probably been burning for thousands of years," Randy remarked, "ever since the first Martians built the city."

"It'll probably be thousands of years more before it'll go out," Ted added. "It seems to have the natural light that Mr. Garland said some of the Martian caves have."

They paused before a statue, and all three of them felt chills race up their backs as they realized they were the first Earth humans ever to gaze on the true likeness of a Martian. The man was not very different from Earthmen. He had the usual number of arms and legs, but he was short and spindly and his head was bald. If the color of the statue was correct, the extinct Martians had light-green skins.

"Dad and the other scientists will sure have the time of their lives with this place!" Ted said. "It may even hold the answer to the biggest riddle about what caused the Martians to disappear."

"Father won't find out anything about it if we don't get out of here!" Jill said anxiously.

"There must be a way to the top of the ground somewhere," Randy answered. "I don't see how the Martians could have walked up that steep incline we slid down."

"Maybe the dirt has covered it over during the years," Ted said. "Maybe there are steps underneath. But I don't see how we could expect to uncover them. Let's go on."

They moved along, searching the uneven rocky streets. It was not a large city, and the three had no trouble keeping their bearings.

A check on their air supply showed only an hour and a half of oxygen left in each of their suits. There would be even less were they to hurry and so breathe faster. This time they had no spare cartridges. If they did not find their way topside by that time, they were surely doomed.

After covering part of the city, the children found that the end of it fanned out into five separate narrow streets.

"One of these streets may lead to ground level," Ted said.

237

"The only thing to do is try them," Randy came back.

"We'll save time if each of us takes a different way," Ted suggested.

But Jill would have none of this plan. She had no desire to follow a lonely underground avenue by herself. They finally decided that Ted and Jill would go together and Randy agreed to go alone.

"We've got to watch out that we don't get lost," Ted cautioned. "Don't go off down any alleyways, Randy. We won't either."

"We ought to set a time when we both meet back here," Randy said.

"I've got it," Ted said. "We'll count off ten minutes and then start heading back whether we've found anything or not. If neither of us has found anything, we'll try the other streets the same way."

Ted and Jill took their leave of Randy and set off down the thorofare. They had to hurry because of their dwindling time, and yet they dared not go so fast that they were breathing heavily. The way they followed carried them quite a distance down the deserted street, on both sides of which were crumbling buildings of plaster set close together. By the time the ten minutes was up, Ted and Jill had come to a dead end against a stone wall.

"This way certainly can't help us," Ted muttered. "Let's go back to Randy."

When they got back and Randy had not returned, Ted became worried. Time was fleeting steadily, and they still were no better off than they had been before. Finally Ted heard a scuffling along the street and saw Randy hurrying his way.

"No luck!" he gasped. "I got sidetracked on the way back. Then I had to run to get here in time."

"You shouldn't have done that," Ted told him. "Now you've got less air than we have. What does your gauge show?"

"Fifty-six minutes," Randy answered, after checking.

Ted examined his own and asked Jill about hers. "We've got an hour and five," Ted said.

"We'll have to hurry if we're going to search

the other three streets," Randy pointed out.

This time Jill agreed to help by going alone so as to save time. They agreed to cut the search period to five minutes, at which time they would come back to their meeting place. Ted had been gone about a minute when he heard someone calling. His heart stirred with hope, and he hustled back at moderate speed to the place from where they had started.

"I think I've found a way out!" Jill was crying excitedly.

Fortunately they were able to catch Randy before he got very far, and the two boys followed Jill down the street where she had made her discovery. After a hundred feet or so they came into a big open area and at one side of it there rose a huge stone staircase leading upward.

"There!" Jill cried happily.

"Let's go up!" Ted urged.

They started up the steps that slowly turned in a half spiral as they ascended. After a long climb, the children found themselves in a large gallery. In spite of their hurry, the three became as hypnotized by the sight of many stone tables or altars arranged in orderly fashion throughout the place. Lying on top of the altars were long oblong cases, fancily decorated.

"These must be coffins!" Randy burst out.

"Let's get out of here!" Jill pleaded.

Ted's gaze had turned from the altars to the smooth, rounded walls of the room that were covered with paintings from one end to the other.

"Look!" he exclaimed, running over to the wall. "The Martians had a Michelangelo too! Those pictures seem to tell a story! Say, do you suppose this mural shows the history of the Martian race and what happened to them?"

"I don't care what they show, Ted!" Jill retorted. "All I want to do is get out of here before our air is gone!"

Ted saw the wisdom of her remark and gave up an impulse to look over the exciting story in pictures. Another flight of stairs was the only way out of the shrine, and without delay the three hurried up. They made a final turn on the stairs and then the subdued glare of Martian sunlight struck their faces. They were finally above ground.

They appeared to have walked into a sporting arena which was surrounded by tiers of stone seats, much in the manner of the ancient Roman Coliseum. As the three of them crossed it through deep powdery dust, they found bones of strange animals scattered over the whole area. There were also the remains of curved swords and scarred shields.

"Ugh!" Jill shuddered. "There's no telling what terrible things took place on this very spot we're walking over!"

"There's an opening over there on the other side," Randy indicated.

"Let's go to it," Ted suggested. "I can't wait to get off this gruesome field either!"

They moved across the arena briskly, yet not too fast. They headed directly for the opening in the high stone wall that encircled the ancient field of contest. When they reached the entrance-way, they passed through and found themselves at the fringe of a forest. A few dozen paces carried them through green corkscrew trees to an open plain.

"I guess the trees around here kept this place from being discovered before now," Ted said.

"Which way do we go now?" Jill moaned. "We've got to find that cave where our air tanks are!"

Ted made a quick orientation of their position in relation to the arena and underground city. "My guess is the cave ought to be in that direction," he said, pointing southward around the bend of the arena. "What do you think, Randy?"

"It sounds right," Randy agreed. "Let's get started."

They had no more than set out again when Ted suddenly pulled up sharply in his tracks, nearly toppling over backward in the motion.

"Gee! Look what I almost stepped on!" he shouted, pointing in the dust ahead of him.

It was a matlike object, lying flat in the red dust, with rows and rows of fine hairs vibrating over its surface. Ted remembered the deadly carpet plant from his study of Martian botany in school.

"Ted!" Jill screamed, as she saw the danger.

To study the action of the plant for himself, Ted picked up a broken shard of pottery and tossed it onto the plant. Instantly the voracious plant rolled up tightly, enveloping the shard in its sucking folds.

"That's what would have happened to your foot if you'd stepped on it, Ted," Randy said in a shivery voice.

They carefully skirted the carpet plant and hurried on, bearing southward in the direction they hoped would bring them to the mouth of the cave that had been the original cause of their trouble.

"How much air time, Randy?" Ted asked, beginning to pant a little.

"Eighteen minutes," Randy answered, and Ted could hear a nervous whimper from Jill.

"You sure this is right, Ted?" Randy asked worriedly, a few minutes later. "If you're wrong we'll die. I've only got seven minutes of air left now. It's really going fast with us hurrying so!"

Ted sighed heavily and felt a clutch of dread in his heart as he studied Jill's pinched, anxious expression. They *had* to be headed right! They just couldn't lose the battle after being so close to salvation.

At last they rounded a huge face of rock that Ted thought he remembered. The cave should be only a few feet away beyond that clump of vegetation, he told himself. They pushed through the curling, tubelike leaves. To their left lay the cave entrance!

Randy gave a cry of relief and dashed into the cave. Ted and his sister entered more slowly; they had a little more time to waste than Randy. When they entered, they found Randy hastily discarding his old oxygen cartridge and replacing it with a new one. When he was through, he helped Jill with hers while Ted attended to his own.

When they were done, they sat down on the floor of the cave and drank in deep, refreshing draughts of the precious gas they had feared they would never breathe again.

"Isn't this great?" Ted remarked. "Just like a cold drink on a hot day!"

"Speaking of food, I could use some," Jill said. "I'm starved after all that!"

"Let's go back and get it," Randy proposed. "We dropped the food case when the elephant ant was chasing us."

"Do you think it's safe?" Jill asked.

"If it's the ant you're afraid of, they do most of their hunting at night," Randy reassured her. "I don't think there's much chance of meeting it."

They started out over the trail they had followed in such haste the night before. After a while they found their food case where they had dropped it. All made a run for it at the same time. The sight of food settled their nerves, and they ate nearly all of the supply in the case. When they were through, Randy happened to look up into the distance and jabbed Ted in the ribs.

"Look!" he exclaimed. "Somebody's coming!"

Ted and Jill leaped to their feet. They shaded

their eyes with their gloved hands in order to see better.

"It's the search party!" Ted burst out.

"Father's with them!" Jill said joyfully.

"I can see Pops too!" came from Randy.

Ted uttered a deep, long sigh. Their frightening adventure was over at last.

CHAPTER TWENTY-TWO

Of Days to Come

THE KENTONS had just risen from the supper table after a wonderful meal that had featured fresh fruits and vegetables from their own garden. Two days had passed since the adventure in the Great Martian Forest. This was a night of celebration, and Mr. Matthews was present.

"Now tell us the surprise you had for us, Father," Jill begged, as they all sat in the living room together. Mrs. Kenton had left cleaning up until later in order to be in on the exciting talk of the evening.

"Not until I know for sure," Dr. Kenton replied. "I'll get a phone call in a few minutes about it."

"Can't you even tell us what it's *about?*" Jill went on.

"I wouldn't want to build up false hopes for nothing, Jill," her father said. "You can wait a little while."

"It was a privilege to eat in such celebrated company tonight," Mr. Matthews said, with a wink at the children. "You kids will even get your name in the schoolbooks for finding that fabulous city."

"It's the pilot and Mr. Garland who got us to bail out that should get the credit," Ted said, with a grin. "If it weren't for them, we'd never have found the underground city."

"The mural showing the great events in the lives of the ancient Martians was the most important thing of all," Dr. Kenton remarked. "I was beginning to believe that the greatest riddle of Mars was never going to be solved." Dr. Kenton had gone to the underground city as soon as he met the young explorers and had heard about their outstanding discovery.

Ted, Jill, and Randy knew the answer now, as did every other colonist on the red planet. The paintings on the wall of the shrine had revealed the baffling riddle. It was simply and clearly portrayed in pictures, just as though the Martians had expected someone someday to know their story. The revelation was that hundreds of years ago all Martians had left their world in large space ships because of Mars's disappearing oxygen. Apparently there still existed somewhere the remains of a supercivilization which had built these space craft.

"Do you think the animals on Mars will finally die out, Dad?" Ted asked, "as the rest of the oxygen combines with the rocks?"

"Eventually, I would think," Dr. Kenton replied.

"Where do you suppose the Martians went to find a new home?" Mr. Matthews asked.

"They may still be looking," the scientist replied. "It's a long way to the stars, remember, and we're sure they didn't land any place in our solar system."

Just then, Yank came bounding into the room.

He too had been permitted inside for the celebration. He had been eating his supper in the kitchen. Ted was amazed to see the color bear run up to his father and stand beside him while the scientist scratched his head.

"You and Yank are friends!" Ted exclaimed.

"We sure are," Dr. Kenton said. "After you kids left, poor Yank was so lonely he even turned to me. I guess he decided to bury the hatchet when he found out I meant him no harm."

"I wonder why he was so long making friends," Jill remarked.

Dr. Kenton took one of Yank's forepaws and rubbed back the fur, revealing a scar. "Yank is the fellow I hurt accidentally a few years ago," the scientist said. "I just thought of checking his paw the day you kids left on your trip."

"He never forgot, did he?" Jill asked.

"Not until I'd convinced him I was sorry," her father replied, rumpling the soft hair of the bear's head. "His injury was the reason he was alone in the world. He couldn't keep up with the pace of his friends."

"Our family is so safe and cozy here," Mrs.

Kenton said, "I hate to think of you going out into that cold wilderness again on a new expedition, John."

"Maybe I won't be going," Dr. Kenton said, with a mysterious smile.

"What do you mean?" his wife asked in surprise.

Just then the phone buzzed. Dr. Kenton went into the hall to answer it. In a few moments he was back again, and he was smiling happily.

"Kids, how would you like to go back to Earth at the end of the school term?" he asked the children.

"Gee, do you mean that?" Ted exclaimed.

"Oh, Father!" Jill cried out joyously.

"It's true enough," their father said. "That's what the call was about and the surprise I was hoping to have for you."

"That's the grandest surprise you could have had," Mrs. Kenton murmured, unspeakably happy herself.

"The Science Union has offered this trip to you, Jill, you, Randy, and you, Ted, as a reward for your important discovery," Dr. Kenton went

They grabbed Yank's paws and began dancing.

on. "They also want me to go back and give lectures all over the country on our latest findings about Mars. It may keep me there a long time."

"That's wonderful!" Mrs. Kenton said. "I was afraid you'd have to stay behind here."

Ted and Jill were so enthusiastic over the proposed trip that they grabbed Yank's paws and began dancing around with him. Randy stood watching them, not quite sharing their high spirits. When Ted saw him, he grabbed Randy's hand and made him join in the celebration. A moment later Randy was enjoying himself as much as the rest.

Dr. Kenton said to Randy's father: "They are in need of some space-port engineers back on Earth. If Randy would like to go with Ted and Jill, would you consider a job like that?"

"You may not know it, John, but I've had my application in for such a job for years," Mr. Matthews answered, highly pleased. "I'll say I'll take it!"

"If you kids will stop jumping around a minute," Dr. Kenton said, "I've got something else to say."

They stopped and listened intently.

"If we go Earthward it may be a long time before we come back to Mars," he said. "We—or at least you—may never get back."

"That's all right with me," Ted said. "I've seen enough of Mars to last me a lifetime! It's interesting here, but it's nothing compared to good old Earth."

"That's what I say!" Jill chimed in.

"There's more here that I should like to look into," the scientist said, with a brooding look on his face. "There are still many unsolved mysteries, such as how these great canals were built, and I'd like to be in on the discovery—if and when it's ever made."

"We can take Yank home with us to Virginia, can't we?" Jill asked anxiously.

"I don't see why not," Dr. Kenton answered. "He seemed to adapt himself to our breathing mixture all right."

Jill hugged the little Martian animal and got a grateful lick in return. Then the Kenton children took Randy aside and began telling him of the wonders of Earth that he would soon be able to see for himself.

"Wait until you enjoy the fun of a swim on a hot day!" Ted said.

"—And the cold air turning your nose red in the winter and the crunch of snow under your feet!" Jill put in.

"It sounds great," Randy said, his eyes sparkling with anticipation. "I think I'm going to like Earth."

"I know you will," Ted said earnestly. "There's nothing as wonderful as Earth in all the universe!"

It looked as though Ted's trip to Mars would turn out to be nothing more than a long visit. A few weeks from now he would be a traveler returning home to his beloved land. What wondrous stories he'd tell the kids back there of adventure on the mysterious red planet which hung in the deeps of everlasting night!

THE END